EX LIBRIS

VINTAGE **CLASSICS**

NOTES FROM UNDERGROUND

Born in Moscow in 1821, Fyodor Mikhaylovich Dostoevsky is regarded as one of the greatest writers who ever lived. Literary modernism and various schools of psychology and theology have been deeply changed by his ideas. He died in 1881 in St Petersburg, Russia.

Richard Pevear has published translations of Alain Yves Bonnefoy, Alberto Savinio and Pavel Florensky, as well as two books of poetry. He has received fellowships for translation from the National Endowment for the Arts, the Ingram Merrill Foundation, the Guggenheim Foundation, and a grant from the National Endowment for the Humanities in support of the translation of *The Brothers Karamazov*.

Larissa Volokhonsky was born in Leningrad. She has translated the work of the prominent Orthodox theologians Alexander Schmemann and John Meyendorff.

Together Richard Pevear and Larissa Volokhonsky have translated Tolstoy's *War and Peace* and *The Death of Ivan Ilyich and Other Stories*, available from Vintage Classics.

ALSO BY FYODOR DOSTOEVSKY

The Brothers Karamazov
Crime and Punishment
Demons

FYODOR DOSTOEVSKY

Notes from Underground

TRANSLATED AND ANNOTATED BY
Richard Pevear and
Larissa Volokhonsky

VINTAGE BOOKS
London

Published by Vintage 2006

20

This translation has been made from the Russian text of
the Soviet Academy of Sciences edition, volume five
(Leningrad, 1973)

A portion of this work was originally published in *Epoch*

First published by Alfred Knopf Inc.

First published by Vintage in 1993

Vintage
Random House, 20 Vauxhall Bridge Road,
London SW1V 2SA

www.vintage-classics.info

Addresses for companies within The Random House Group Limited
can be found at: www.randomhouse.co.uk/offices.htm

The Random House Group Limited Reg. No. 954009

A CIP catalogue record for this book
is available from the British Library

ISBN 9780099140115

Penguin Random House is committed to a sustainable future for
our business, our readers and our planet. This book is made from
Forest Stewardship Council® certified paper.

Printed and bound in Great Britain by Clays Ltd, Elcograf S.p.A.

Contents

Contents

Foreword

THE ELLIPSIS after the opening sentence of *Notes from Underground* is like a window affording us a first glimpse of one of the most remarkable characters in literature, one who has been placed among the bearers of modern consciousness alongside Don Quixote, Hamlet, and Faust. What we see is a man glancing at us out of the corner of his eye, very much aware of us as he speaks, very much concerned with the impression his words are making. In fact, we do not really see him, we only hear him, and not through anything so respectable as a window, but through a crack in the floorboards. He addresses the world from that crack; he has also spent a lifetime listening at it. Everything that can be said about him, and more particularly against him, he already knows; he has, as he says in a typical paradox, overheard it all, anticipated it all, invented it all. "I am a sick man . . . I am a wicked man." In the space of that pause Dostoevsky introduces the unifying idea of his tale: the instability, the perpetual "dialectic" of isolated consciousness.

The nameless hero—nameless "because 'I' is all of us," the critic Viktor Shklovsky suggested—is, like so many of Dostoevsky's heroes, a writer. Not a professional man of letters (none of Dostoevsky's "writers" is that), but one whom circumstances have led or forced to take up the pen, to try to fix something in words, for his own sake first of all, but also with an eye for some indeterminate *others*—readers, critics, judges, fellow creatures. He is a passionate amateur, a condition that marks the style and structure as well as the content of the book. Where the master practitioner would present us with a seamless and harmonious verbal construction, the man from underground, who literally cannot contain himself, breaks decorum all the time, interrupts himself, comments on his own intentions, defies his readers, polemicizes with other writers. The literariness of his "notes" and the unliterariness of his style are both results of his "heightened consciousness," his hostility to and dependence upon the words of others. Thus the unifying idea of *Notes from Underground*, embodied in the person of its narrator, is dramatized in the process of its writing. The controlling art of Dostoevsky remains at a second remove.

This man who may be trying to write his way out of the underground, originally read his way into it. "At home," he says, "I mainly used to read. I wished to stifle with external sensations all that was ceaselessly boiling up inside me. And among external sensations the only one possible for me was reading. Reading was, of course, a great help—it stirred, delighted, and tormented me." That was during his youth, in the 1840s. He read, he dreamed, and he engaged in "little debauches." These were his three diversions, and it is interesting that he puts them together. What did he read? At various points in his account he compares himself with Byron's Manfred, with characters from Pushkin and Lermontov—all romantic figures. He refers more than once to Rousseau. Farther in the background, but looming large, stand Kant and Schiller, representing German philosophical and poetic idealism, summoned up in the phrase "the beautiful and lofty," which had become a commonplace of Russian liberal criticism of the 1840s. His reading was, in other words, that of the typical educated Russian of the time. Reading nourished his dreaming, and even found its way into his little debauches "in exactly the proportion required for a good sauce." And so it was that he evaded the petty squalor and inner anguish of his daily life; so it was, as he confesses sixteen years later, that he "defaulted on his life through moral corruption in a corner." One main thematic strand of the book is the underground man's denunciation of the estranging and vitiating influence of books, so that from his perspective of the 1860s, when he begins to write, the word "literary" has become one of the most sarcastic he can utter. To all the features for an antihero purposely collected in *Notes from Underground* there are added all the features for an antibook.

That book is the underground man's book, not Dostoevsky's, though the two coincide almost word for word. Indeed, the sharp personality of the underground man, the intensity of his attacks and confessions, the apparent lack of critical distance in the first person narrative, have given many readers the impression that they have to do here with a direct statement of Dostoevsky's own ideological position, and much commentary has been written on the book in that light. Much has also been said about the tragic (or at least "terribly sad") essence of its vision. Both notions seem to overlook the humor—stylistic, situational, polemical, parodic—that pervades *Notes from Underground*. Dostoevsky certainly put a lot of himself into the situations and emotions of his narrator; what distinguishes his book from the narrator's is an extra dimension of laughter. Laughter creates the distance that allows for recognition, without which the book might be a tract, a case history, a cry of despair, anything you like, but not a work of art. *Notes from Underground* has been called the prelude to the great novels of Dostoevsky's last period, and it is so partly because here Dostoevsky first perfected the method of tonal distancing that enabled him to present characters and events simultaneously from different points of view, to counter empathy with intellection.

The underground man's book is a personal outpouring—harsh, self-accusatory, defiant, negligently written, loosely structured—a long diatribe, followed by some avowedly random recollections ("I will not introduce any order or system. Whatever I recall, I will write down.") It claims to be *genuine*, if artistically crude. "No longer literature, but corrective punishment," the narrator finally decides. Nietzsche thought he could hear "the voice of the blood" in it.

Dostoevsky's novel is something quite different. It is a tragicomedy of ideas, admirable for the dramatic expressiveness of its prose, which gives subtle life to this voice from under the floorboards with all its withholdings, second thoughts, loopholes, special pleadings; and admirable, too, for the dynamics of its composition, the interplay of its two parts, which represent two historical moments, two "climates of opinion," as well as two images of the man from underground, revealed by different means and with very different tonalities.

The two parts of *Notes from Underground* were first published in 1864, in the January and April issues of *Epoch*, a magazine edited by Dostoevsky's brother Mikhail, the successor to their magazine *Time*, which had been suppressed by the censors in 1863. The note Dostoevsky added to the first part insists on the social and typical, as opposed to personal and psychological, aspects of the man from underground: "such persons as the writer of such notes not only may but even must exist in our society, taking into consideration the circumstances under which our society has generally been formed." His view of those circumstances would have been familiar to readers of his articles in *Time* over the previous few years, particularly "Winter Notes on Summer Impressions," an account of his first trip to Europe in 1862, which had appeared in the February and March issues of *Time* for

1863. There he discussed Russia's "captivation" with the West:

> Why, everything, unquestionably almost everything that
> we have—of development, science, art, civic-mindedness,
> humanity, everything, everything comes from there—
> from that same land of holy wonders! Why, our entire
> life, even from very childhood itself, has been set up
> along European lines.

Russian society had been formed by decades of imported "development" and "enlightenment," words that acquire a sharply ironic inflection in Dostoevsky's later work. Some sources of this ideology have already been mentioned—Rousseau, Schiller, Kant. To this list may be added the names of such French social romantics as Victor Hugo, Eugène Sue, George Sand, and the utopian socialists Fourier and Saint-Simon. In *Dostoevsky: The Stir of Liberation*, Joseph Frank points to the presence of these "influences" in the theme of the redeemed prostitute, which was a favorite among Russian liberals of the 1840s (the poet Nikolai Nekrasov, for example), and which Dostoevsky parodies brilliantly in the second part of *Notes from Underground*. The parody is, of course, Dostoevsky's, not the underground man's. The latter, on the contrary, had taken all these influences to heart; they had made him into a "developed man of the nineteenth century," a man of "heightened consciousness." It was the attempt to live by them that drove him "underground." In the social displacement of an imported culture, Dostoevsky perceived a more profound human displacement, a spiritual void filled with foreign content.

A second theme from "Winter Notes" reappears in *Notes from Underground*—that of the "crystal palace," which is as central to the polemics of the novel's first part as the redeemed prostitute is to the parody of the second. The crystal palace in the travel article is the cast-iron and glass exhibition hall built in London in 1851 for the Great Exhibition. It appeared to Dostoevsky as a terrifying structure, a symbol of false unity, of "the full triumph of Baal, the ultimate organization of an anthill." The tones in which he speaks of it will be echoed almost twenty years later by the Grand Inquisitor in *The Brothers Karamazov*:

> But if you saw how proud is that mighty spirit who created this colossal setting and how proudly convinced this spirit is of its victory and of its triumph, then you would shudder for its pride, obstinacy, and blindness, but you would shudder also for those over whom this proud spirit hovers and reigns.

This mighty spirit is the spirit of industrial capitalism, and the crystal palace is its temple. In *Notes from Underground* the same structure comes to stand for the future organization of socialism. It remains an image of false unity, but is denounced in rather different terms: the underground man puts his tongue out at it, calls it a tenement house and a chicken coop.

The two time periods of the novel represent two stages in the evolution of the Russian intelligentsia: the sentimental, literary 1840s and the rational and utilitarian 1860s; the time of the liberals and the time of the nihilists. One of Dostoevsky's constant preoccupations in his later work was the responsibility of the liberal generation for the emergence of the nihilists, an idea he embodied literally in the novel *Demons* (1871–72) in the figures of the dreamy individualist Stepan Verkhovensky and his deadly utilitarian son Pyotr. In *Notes from Underground* the same evolution is reflected in the mind of one man: the polemicist of the first part grew out of the defeated dreamer of the second. The inverted time sequence of the two parts seems to lead us to this discovery.

However, the underground man is hardly a typical "rational egoist," any more than he had been a typical romantic. There is a quality in him that sets him apart, which he himself defines on the last page of the book: "Excuse me, gentlemen, but I am not justifying myself with this *allishness*. As far as I myself am concerned, I have merely carried to an extreme in my life what you have not dared to carry even halfway." Submitted to the testing of full acceptance, the testing of this irreducible human existence, the "heightened consciousness" of the rationalist, like the sentimental impulses of the romantic, runs into disastrous and comic reversals. Hence the paradoxically defiant double-mindedness of the underground man, and his intransitive dilemma.

The "gentlemen" he addresses throughout his notes, when they are not a more indeterminate "you," are typical intellectuals of the 1860s. More specifically, they are presumed to be followers of the writer Nikolai Gavrilovich Chernyshevsky, the chief spokesman and ideologist of the young radicals. N. G. Chernyshevsky was the author of a number of critical works, notably *The Anthropological Principle in Philosophy* (1860), in which he propounded the abovementioned doctrine of "rational egoism," an adaptation of the "enlightened self-interest" of the English utilitarians. His programmatic utopian novel *What Is to Be Done?*, written in prison following his arrest in 1862 for revolutionary activities and published in 1863, immediately became a manual for social activists. Several decades later, V. I. Lenin, who dubbed Dostoevsky a "superlatively bad" writer, could testify that *What Is to Be Done?* had made him into a confirmed revolutionary. The nature of Chernyshevsky's hero and his ideas may be deduced from the following passage:

Yes, I will always do what I want. I will never sacrifice anything, not even a whim, for the sake of something I do not desire. What I want, with all my heart, is to make people happy. In this lies my happiness. Mine! Can you hear that, you, in your underground hole?

This is the voice of the healthy rational egoist, the ingenuous man of action. Dostoevsky took up the challenge.

Though Chernyshevsky is not mentioned by name in *Notes from Underground*, his theories, and in particular his novel, are the most immediate targets both of the underground man's diatribes and of Dostoevsky's subtler, more penetrating parody. Dostoevsky had intended originally to write a critical review of *What Is to Be Done?* for the first issue of *Epoch*, but was unable to produce anything. The strained conditions of his personal life at that time and the problems of starting the new magazine do not explain the difficulty he faced. Evidently it was not enough for him simply to counter Chernyshevsky's arguments; more was at stake than a conflict of ideas—there was a question of the very nature of the human being who was to be so forcibly made happy. Dostoevsky's response had to take artistic form. He was challenged to reveal "the man in man," precisely in and through the ideas of the new radicals themselves.

The counterarguments of the "gentlemen" in the later chapters of the first part, for example, are clearly Chernyshevskian, based on his notions of normal interests, natural law, and the denial of free will. The crystal palace, too, in its reappearance here, has been transmuted by its passage through "The Fourth Dream of Vera Pavlovna," the section of *What Is to Be Done?* that presents Chernyshevsky's vision of mankind made happy. The pseudoscientific terms and even a certain clumsy use of parentheses, as Joseph Frank has shown, are the narrator's deliberate mockery of Chernyshevsky's writing. Frank has also shown that the attack is not limited to Part I: two of the three main episodes in the second part of *Notes*—the episode of the bumped officer and the episode with the prostitute Liza—are in fact parodic developments of episodes from Chernyshevsky's novel. The latter episode, which is the climactic episode of the novel as a whole, gives fullest play to Dostoevsky's criticism through comic reversal. But the reversal is not a simple contrary; it is the puncturing of a literary cliché by a truth drawn from a different source, from what the narrator comes in the end to call "living life."

Dostoevsky's reply to Chernyshevsky is both ideological and artistic, the implication being that the two are inseparable, and the further implication being that the indispensable unity of artistic form reflects a more primordial unity of the living person. Those who favored Chernyshevsky's ideas, however, were able to separate them from the form of their expression. Even the conscientious old radical Alexander Herzen, though he found Chernyshevsky's novel "vilely written" and could not help noting that it ends with "a phalanstery in a brothel," immediately added: "On the other hand there is much that is good and healthy." (An interesting pair of adjectives when one recalls the opening lines of *Notes*.) These remarks of Herzen's are passed on to us by Fyodor Godunov-Cherdyntsev, the narrator of Vladimir Nabokov's *The Gift* (1938), whose monograph on the life of Chernyshevsky makes up the fourth of the novel's five chapters. Godunov-Cherdyntsev notes a certain "fatal inner contradiction" in Chernyshevsky's own reflections on art, what he describes as

the dualism of the monist Chernyshevsky's aesthetics—where "form" and "content" are distinct, with "content" pre-eminent—or, more exactly, with "form" playing the role of the soul and "content" the role of the body; and the muddle is augmented by the fact that this "soul" consists of mechanical components, since Chernyshevsky believed that the value of a work was not a qualitative but a quantitative concept, and that "if someone were to take some miserable, forgotten novel and carefully cull all its flashes of observation, he would collect a fair number of sentences that would not differ in worth from those constituting the pages of works we admire."

Indeed, there could hardly be a more thorough denial of artistic unity than this last quoted passage. The naïve blitheness of its expression is characteristic of Chernyshevsky and thinkers like him (utilitarians, nihilists; then Lenin, Lunacharsky, the theorists of "socialist realism"). It is defined by Nabokov's narrator in terms of a decomposition of the human person. The metaphor comes quite naturally; the aesthetic question immediately brings with it the human question—or, rather, they are the same.

As a writer and thinker, Chernyshevsky was the embodiment of what in Russian is called *bezdarnost'*—giftlessness—and was thus the perfect foil for that minutely observant, wondering, grateful, and form-revealing intelligence that Nabokov celebrates in *The Gift*. Giftlessness, as Dostoevsky feared and Nabokov knew, became the dominant style in Russia; it eventually seized power, and in the process of "making people happy" destroyed them by millions, leaving its vast motherland broken and desolate. "The triumph of materialism has abolished matter," the poet Andrei Bely said in the famine-ridden 1920s. Godunov-Cherdyntsev gives a more detailed formulation:

Our overall impression is that materialists of this type fell into a fatal error: neglecting the nature of the thing itself, they kept applying their most materialistic method merely to the relations between objects, to the void between objects and not to the objects themselves; i.e. they were the naïvest metaphysicians precisely at that point where they most wanted to be standing on the ground.

A fatal error, a fatal contradiction. In this respect the greatest foresight was shown by long-eared Shigalyov, the radical theoretician in Dostoevsky's *Demons*: "I got entangled in my own data, and my conclusion directly contradicts the original idea I start from. Starting from unlimited freedom, I conclude with unlimited despotism. I will add, however, that apart from my solution to the social formula, there is no other." A direct line leads from metaphysical naïvety to murder; a direct line leads from the anti-unity of utilitarian aesthetics to the false unity of the crystal palace. Dostoevsky perceived these relations more clearly than anyone else of his time. The perception coincided with, and in fact constituted, the maturity of his genius. He recognized that his opposition to the "Chernyshevskians" could not be a struggle for domination, that what was in question was the complex reality of the human being, the whole person, the "thing itself," and that a true articulation of that reality could only come as the final "gift" of an artistic image. Mikhail Bakhtin noted in his study of Dostoevsky's poetics: "Artistic form, correctly understood, does not shape already prepared and found content, but rather permits content to be found and seen for the first time."

Hence the formal inventiveness of *Notes from Underground*: its striking language, unlike any literary prose ever written; its multiple and conflicting tonalities; the oddity of its reversed structure, which seems random but all at once reveals its deeper coherence—"chatter . . . resolved by an unexpected catastrophe," as Dostoevsky described it to his brother. ("All Dostoevsky's novels were written for the sake of the catastrophe," the critic Konstantin Mochulsky observed. "This is the law of the new 'expressive art' that he created. Only upon arriving at the finale do we understand the composition's perfection and the inexhaustible depth of its design.") The catastrophe that resolves *Notes from Underground*, with its resoundingly symbolic slamming door, is at the same time the moment of its origin. There, in a sudden confusion of tenses, the narrator cries out from the past into the future: "and never, never will I recall this moment with indifference." It is a fleeting moment, but it has determined the narrator's life and gives the edge of passion to his attack, his outburst, after all his years "underground." Coming at the end of the book, it sends us back to the beginning; thus the round of the underground man's ruminations is given form, and this whole "image" Dostoevsky holds up to us as a sign.

There may, however, have been a more directly opposing *idea* in the book as Dostoevsky originally wrote it, a sort of ideological climax in Part I to match the narrative climax in Part II. When the first part appeared in *Epoch*, Dostoevsky complained in a letter to his brother that the tenth chapter— "the most important one, where the essential thought is expressed"—had been drastically cut by the censors. "Where I mocked at everything and sometimes blasphemed for form's sake—that is let pass; but where from all this I deduced the need of faith and Christ—that is suppressed."

The published version of the chapter, according to its author, was left "full of self-contradictions." Indeed, the reader will notice that in the third paragraph the "crystal edifice" ceases all at once to represent the ideas of the narrator's opponents and becomes instead something that he himself has possibly invented "as a result of certain old nonrational habits of our generation," something, he says, that "exists in my desires, or, better, exists as long as my desires exist." Obviously there have been major cuts here, removing the transition from one crystal edifice to the other—the word "mansion" being left us as a clue to its nature. We must try to imagine what would have transformed the "chicken coop" into a mansion, what would have made it more than "a phalanstery in a brothel," what would have turned it from an embodiment of the "laws of nature" into a contradiction of those very laws, and how from all this "the need of faith and Christ" was deduced. Dostoevsky never restored the cuts, as he never restored similarly drastic cuts in *Crime and Punishment* and *Demons*. Various explanations have been offered for this circumstance, some practical (lack of time, reluctance to confront the censors), others aesthetic (a recognition that the cuts were improvements). We do not know. But if we look at Dostoevsky's outlines of his ideas for novels in his notebooks and letters and then at the novels themselves, we will realize at least that the scheme barely hints at the surprises of its development. However it was that Dostoevsky "deduced the need for faith and Christ" in this chapter, we may be sure that he did not add it on as an external "ideological" precept, but drew it from the materials of the work itself.

The man from underground refutes his opponents with the results of having carried their own ideas to an extreme in his life. These results are *himself*. This self, however, as the reader discovers at once, is not a monolithic personality, but an inner plurality in constant motion. The plurality of the person, without any ideological additions, is already a refutation of *l'homme de la nature et de la vérité*, the healthy, undivided man of action who was both the instrument and the object of radical social theory. Unity is not singularity but wholeness, a holding together, a harmony, all of which imply plurality. What the principle of this harmony is, the underground man cannot say; he has never found it. But he *knows* he has not found it; he knows, because his inner disharmony, his dividedness, which is the source of his suffering, is also the source of consciousness. Here we come upon one of the deep springs of Dostoevsky's later work—not his thinking (Dostoevsky was not a thinker, or, rather, he was a plurality of thinkers), but his artistic embodiment of reality. The one quality his negative characters share, and almost the only negative his world view allows, is inner fixity, a sort of death-in-life, which can take many forms and tonalities, from the broadly comic to the tragic, from the mechanical to the corpselike, from Pyotr Petrovich Luzhin to Nikolai Stavrogin. Inner movement, on the other hand, is always a condition of spiritual good, though it may also be a source of suffering, division, disharmony, in this life. What moves may always rise. Dostoevsky never portrays the completion of this movement; it extends beyond the end of the given book. We see it in characters like Raskolnikov and Mitya Karamazov, but first of all in the man from underground.

* * *

> How much the mere tone of *Notes from Underground* is worth!
>
> LEV SHESTOV

THE PHILOSOPHER SHESTOV, the critic Mochulsky, and most Russian readers agree that the style of *Notes from Underground* is, in Shestov's words, "very strange." Bakhtin describes it as "deliberately clumsy," though "subject to a certain artistic logic." A detailed discussion of the matter is not possible here, but we can offer a few comments on the style of our translation, pointing to qualities in the original that we have sought to keep in English for the sake of "mere tone," where they have been lost in earlier translations.

Though he likes to philosophize, the underground man has

no use for philosophical terminology. When he picks up such words, it is to make fun of them; otherwise he couches his thought in the most blunt and even crude terms. An example is his use of the rare word *khoténiye*, a verbal noun formed from *khotét'*, "to want." It is a simple, elemental word, with an almost physical, appetitive immediacy. The English equivalent is "wanting," which is how we have translated it. The primitive quality of the word appears to have alarmed our predecessors, who translate it as "wishing," "desire," "will," "intention," "choice," "volition," and render it variously at various times. The underground man invariably says "wanting" and "to want." He plays on the different uses of the word ("Who wants to want according to a little table?"); there is one passage running from the end of Chapter VII to the start of Chapter VIII in the first part where "want" and "wanting" appear eighteen times in two paragraphs—the stylistic point of which is blunted when other words are used.

Another of the underground man's words is *výgoda*, which means "profit" (gain, benefit), and only secondarily "advantage," as it is most often translated. "Profit" has very nearly the same range of uses in English as *výgoda* has in Russian. It is also a direct, unambiguous word, with an almost tactile quality: you *have* an advantage, but you *get* a profit. And like *výgoda*, with its strongly accented first syllable, "profit" leaps from the mouth almost with the force of an expletive, quite unlike the more unctuous "advantage" or its Russian equivalent *preimúshchestvo*. Again, the narrator insists on his word and plays with it. Thus we arrive at the full music of this underground oratorio:

And where did all these sages get the idea that man needs some normal, some virtuous wanting? What made them necessarily imagine that what man needs is necessarily a reasonably profitable wanting? Man needs only independent wanting, whatever this independence may cost and wherever it may lead.

Repetition is of the essence here. When the underground man speaks of consciousness and heightened consciousness, it is always the same word: "consciousness," not "intellectual activity" as one translator has it, not "awareness" as another offers, and never some mixture of the three. The editorial precept of avoiding repetitions, of gracefully varying one's vocabulary, cannot be applied to this writer. His writing is emphatic, heavy-handed, rude: "This is my wanting, this is my desire. You will scrape it out of me only when you change my desires." To translate the scullery verb *výskoblit'* ("to scrape out") as "eradicate" or "expunge," as has been done, to exchange the "collar of lard" the narrator bestows on the wretched clerk in Part II for one that is merely "greasy," is to chasten and thus distort the voice of this man who is nothing but a voice.

There is, however, one tradition of mistranslation attached to *Notes from Underground* that raises something more than a question of "mere tone." The second sentence of the book, *Ya zloy chelovék*, has most often been rendered as "I am a spiteful man." *Zloy* is indeed at the root of the Russian word for "spiteful" (*zlóbnyi*), but it is a much broader and deeper word, meaning "wicked," "bad," "evil." The wicked witch in Russian folktales is *zláya véd'ma* (*zláya* being the feminine of *zloy*). The opposite of *zloy* is *dóbryi*, "good," as in "good fairy" (*dóbraya féya*). This opposition is of great importance for *Notes from Underground*; indeed it frames the book, from "I am a wicked man" at the start to the outburst close to the end: "They won't let me . . . I can't be . . . good!" We can talk forever about the inevitable loss of nuances in translating from Russian into English (or from any language into any other), but the translation of *zloy* as "spiteful" instead of "wicked" is not inevitable, nor is it a matter of nuance. It speaks for that habit of substituting the psychological for the moral, of interpreting a spiritual condition as a kind of behavior, which has so bedeviled our century, not least in its efforts to understand Dostoevsky. Besides, "wicked" has the lucky gift of picking up the internal rhyme in the first two sentences of the original.

—RICHARD PEVEAR

NOTES FROM UNDERGROUND

I

Underground*

I

I AM A SICK MAN . . . I am a wicked man. An unattractive man. I think my liver hurts. However, I don't know a fig about my sickness, and am not sure what it is that hurts me. I am not being treated and never have been, though I respect medicine and doctors. What's more, I am also superstitious in the extreme; well, at least enough to respect medicine. (I'm sufficiently educated not to be superstitious, but I am.) No, sir, I refuse to be treated out of wickedness. Now, you will certainly not be so good as to understand this. Well, sir, but I understand it. I will not, of course, be able to explain to you precisely who is going to suffer in this case from my wickedness; I know perfectly well that I will in no way "muck things up" for the doctors by not taking their treatment; I know bet-

*Both the author of the notes and the *Notes* themselves are, of course, fictional. Nevertheless, such persons as the writer of such notes not only may but even must exist in our society, taking into consideration the circumstances under which our society has generally been formed. I wished to bring before the face of the public, a bit more conspicuously than usual, one of the characters of a time recently passed. He is one representative of a generation that is still living out its life. In this fragment, entitled "Underground," this person introduces himself, his outlook, and seeks, as it were, to elucidate the reasons why he appeared and had to appear among us. In the subsequent fragment will come this person's actual "notes" about certain events in his life.

—Fyodor Dostoevsky

ter than anyone that by all this I am harming only myself and no one else. But still, if I don't get treated, it is out of wickedness. My liver hurts; well, then let it hurt even worse!

I've been living like this for a long time—about twenty years. I'm forty now. I used to be in the civil service; I no longer am. I was a wicked official. I was rude, and took pleasure in it. After all, I didn't accept bribes, so I had to reward myself at least with that. (A bad witticism, but I won't cross it out. I wrote it thinking it would come out very witty; but now, seeing for myself that I simply had a vile wish to swagger—I purposely won't cross it out!) When petitioners would come for information to the desk where I sat—I'd gnash my teeth at them, and felt an inexhaustible delight when I managed to upset someone. I almost always managed. They were timid people for the most part: petitioners, you know. But among the fops there was one officer I especially could not stand. He simply refused to submit and kept rattling his sabre disgustingly. I was at war with him over that sabre for a year and a half. In the end, I prevailed. He stopped rattling. However, that was still in my youth. But do you know, gentlemen, what was the main point about my wickedness? The whole thing precisely was, the greatest nastiness precisely lay in my being shamefully conscious every moment, even in moments of the greatest bile, that I was not only not a wicked but was not even an embittered man, that I was simply frightening sparrows in vain, and pleasing myself with it. I'm foaming at the mouth, but bring me some little doll, give me some tea with a bit of sugar, and maybe I'll calm down. I'll even wax tenderhearted, though afterwards I'll certainly gnash my teeth at myself and suffer from insomnia for a few months out of shame. Such is my custom.

And I lied about myself just now when I said I was a wicked official. I lied out of wickedness. I was simply playing around both with the petitioners and with the officer, but as a matter of fact I was never able to become wicked. I was conscious every moment of so very many elements in myself most opposite to that. I felt them simply swarming in me, those opposite elements. I knew they had been swarming in me all my life, asking to be let go out of me, but I would not let them, I would not, I purposely would not let them out. They tormented me to the point of shame; they drove me to convulsions, and—finally I got sick of them, oh, how sick I got! But do you not perhaps think, gentlemen, that I am now repenting of something before you, that I am asking your forgiveness for something? . . . I'm sure you think so . . . However, I assure you that it is all the same to me even if you do . . .

Not just wicked, no, I never even managed to become anything: neither wicked nor good, neither a scoundrel nor an honest man, neither a hero nor an insect. And now I am living out my life in my corner, taunting myself with the spiteful and utterly futile consolation that it is even impossible for an intelligent man seriously to become anything, and only fools become something. Yes, sir, an intelligent man of the nineteenth century must be and is morally obliged to be primarily a characterless being; and a man of character, an active figure—primarily a limited being. This is my forty-year-old conviction. I am now forty years old, and, after all, forty years—is a whole lifetime; after all, it's the most extreme old age. To live beyond forty is indecent, banal, immoral! Who lives beyond forty—answer me sincerely, honestly? I'll tell you who does: fools and scoundrels do. I'll say it in the faces of all the elders, all these venerable elders, all these silver-haired and sweet-smelling elders! I'll say it in the whole world's face! I have the right to speak this way, because I myself will live to be sixty. I'll live to be seventy! I'll live to be eighty! . . . Wait! let me catch my breath . . .

You no doubt think, gentlemen, that I want to make you laugh? Here, too, you're mistaken. I am not at all such a jolly man as you think, or as you possibly think; if, however, irritated by all this chatter (and I already feel you are irritated), you decide to ask me: what precisely am I?—then I will answer you: I am one collegiate assessor.[1] I served so as to have something to eat (but solely for that), and when last year one of my distant relations left me six thousand roubles in his will, I resigned at once and settled into my corner. I lived in this corner before as well, but now I've settled into it. My room is wretched, bad, on the edge of the city. My servant is a village woman, old, wicked from stupidity, and always bad-smelling besides. I'm told that the Petersburg climate is beginning to do me harm, and that with my negligible means life in Petersburg is very expensive. I know all that, I know it better than all these experienced and most wise counsellors and waggers of heads.[2] But I am staying in Petersburg; I will not leave Petersburg! I will not leave because . . . Eh! but it's all completely the same whether I leave or not.

But anyhow: what can a decent man speak about with the most pleasure?

Answer: about himself.

So then I, too, will speak about myself.

I I

I WOULD NOW LIKE to tell you, gentlemen, whether you do or do not wish to hear it, why I never managed to become even an insect. I'll tell you solemnly that I wanted many times to become an insect. But I was not deemed worthy even of that. I swear to you, gentlemen, that to be overly conscious is a sickness, a real, thorough sickness. For man's everyday use, ordinary human consciousness would be more than enough; that is, a half, a quarter of the portion that falls to the lot of a developed man in our unfortunate nineteenth century, who, on top of that, has the added misfortune of residing in Petersburg, the most abstract and intentional city on the entire globe. (Cities can be intentional or unintentional.) As much consciousness, for example, as that by which all so-called ingenuous people and active figures live would be quite enough. I'll bet you think I'm writing all this out of swagger, to be witty at the expense of active figures, and swagger of a bad tone besides, rattling my sabre like my officer. But, gentlemen, who can take pride in his sicknesses, and swagger about them besides?

Though—what am I saying?—everyone does it; it's their sicknesses that everyone takes pride in, and I, perhaps, more than anyone. Let us not argue; my objection was absurd. But all the same I am strongly convinced that not only too much consciousness but even any consciousness at all is a sickness. I stand upon it. But let us also leave that for a moment. Tell me this: why was it that, as if by design, in those same, yes, in those very same moments when I was most capable of being conscious of all the refinements of "everything beautiful and lofty,"³ as we once used to say, it happened that instead of being conscious I did such unseemly deeds, such deeds as . . . well, in short, as everyone does, perhaps, but which with me occurred, as if by design, precisely when I was most conscious that I ought not to be doing them at all? The more conscious I was of the good and of all this "beautiful and lofty," the deeper I kept sinking into my mire, and the more capable I was of getting completely stuck in it. But the main feature was that this was all in me not as if by chance, but as if it had to be so. As if it were my most normal condition and in no way a sickness or a blight, so that finally I lost any wish to struggle against this blight. I ended up almost believing (and maybe indeed believing) that this perhaps was my normal condition. But at first, in the beginning, how much torment I endured in this struggle! I did not believe that such things

happened to others, and therefore kept it to myself all my life
as a secret. I was ashamed (maybe I am ashamed even now);
it reached the point with me where I would feel some secret,
abnormal, mean little pleasure in returning to my corner on
some most nasty Petersburg night and being highly conscious
of having once again done a nasty thing that day, and again
that what had been done could in no way be undone, and I
would gnaw, gnaw at myself with my teeth, inwardly, secret-
ly, tear and suck at myself until the bitterness finally turned
into some shameful, accursed sweetness, and finally—into a
decided, serious pleasure! Yes, a pleasure, a pleasure! I stand
upon it. The reason I've begun to speak is that I keep wanting
to find out for certain: do other people have such pleasures?
I'll explain to you: the pleasure here lay precisely in the too
vivid consciousness of one's own humiliation; in feeling that
one had reached the ultimate wall; that, bad as it is, it cannot
be otherwise; that there is no way out for you, that you will
never change into a different person; that even if you had
enough time and faith left to change yourself into something
different, you probably would not wish to change; and even
if you did wish it, you would still not do anything, because in
fact there is perhaps nothing to change into. And chiefly, and
finally, all this occurs according to the normal and basic laws
of heightened consciousness and the inertia that follows directly from these laws, and consequently there is not only
nothing you can do to change yourself, but there is simply
nothing to do at all. So it turns out, for example, as a result of
heightened consciousness: right, you're a scoundrel—as if it
were a consolation for the scoundrel himself to feel that he is
indeed a scoundrel. But enough . . . Eh, I've poured all that
out, and what have I explained? . . . How explain this pleasure? But I will explain myself! I will carry through to the
end! That is why I took a pen in my hands . . .

I have, for example, a terrible amour propre. I am as inse-
cure and touchy as a hunchback or a dwarf, yet there have
indeed been moments when if I had happened to be slapped,
I might even have been glad of it. I say it seriously: surely I'd
have managed to discover some sort of pleasure in that as
well—the pleasure of despair, of course, but it is in despair that
the most burning pleasures occur, especially when one is all
too highly conscious of the hopelessness of one's position.
And here, with this slap—you'll simply be crushed by the consciousness of what sort of slime you've been reduced to. But
chiefly, however you shuffle, it still comes out that I always
come out as the first to blame for everything and, what's most
offensive, blamelessly to blame, according to the laws of
nature, so to speak. I'm to blame, first, because I'm more
intelligent than everyone around me. (I've always considered
myself more intelligent than everyone around me, and, would
you believe, have even felt slightly ashamed of it. At least I've
somehow averted my eyes all my life, and never could look
people straight in the face.) I'm to blame, finally, because
even if there were any magnanimity in me, I would be the
one most tormented by the consciousness of its utter futility.
For I would surely be able to do nothing with my magnanimity: neither to forgive, because my offender might have hit
me according to the laws of nature, and the laws of nature
cannot be forgiven; nor to forget, because even though it's
the laws of nature, it's still offensive. Finally, even if I should
want to be altogether unmagnanimous, if, on the contrary, I
should wish to take revenge on my offender, I wouldn't be
able to take revenge on anyone in any way, because I surely
wouldn't dare to do anything even if I could. Why wouldn't
I dare? About that I would like to say a couple of words in
particular.

III

WHAT HAPPENS, for example, with people who know how to take revenge and generally how to stand up for themselves? Once they are overcome, say, by vengeful feeling, then for the time there is simply nothing left in their whole being but this feeling. Such a gentleman just lunges straight for his goal like an enraged bull, horns lowered, and maybe only a wall can stop him. (Incidentally: before a wall, these gentlemen—that is, ingenuous people and active figures— quite sincerely fold. For them a wall is not a deflection, as it is, for example, for us, people who think and consequently do nothing; it is not a pretext for turning back, a pretext which our sort usually doesn't believe in but is always very glad to have. No, they fold in all sincerity. For them a wall possesses something soothing, morally resolving and final, perhaps even something mystical . . . But of the wall later.) Well, sirs, it is just such an ingenuous man that I regard as the real, normal man, the way his tender mother—nature—herself wished to see him when she so kindly conceived him on earth. I envy such a man to the point of extreme bile. He is stupid, I won't argue with you about that, but perhaps a normal man ought to be stupid, how do you know? Perhaps it's even very beautiful. And I am the more convinced of this, so to speak, suspicion, seeing that if, for example, one takes the antithesis of the normal man, that is, the man of heightened consciousness, who came, of course, not from the bosom of nature but from a retort (this is almost mysticism, gentlemen, but I suspect that, too), this retort man sometimes folds before his antithesis so far that he honestly regards himself, with all his heightened consciousness, as a mouse and not a man. A highly conscious mouse, perhaps, but a mouse all the same, whereas here we have a man, and consequently . . . and so on . . . And, above all, it is he, he himself, who regards himself as a mouse; no one asks him to; and that is an important point.

Let us now have a look at this mouse in action. Suppose, for example, that it, too, is offended (and it is almost always offended), and it, too, wishes to take revenge. For it may have stored up even more spite than *l'homme de la nature et de la vérité*.[4] The nasty, base little desire to pay the offender back with the same evil may scratch still more nastily in it than in *l'homme de la nature et de la vérité*, because *l'homme de la nature et de la vérité*, with his innate stupidity, regards his revenge quite simply as justice; whereas the mouse, as a result of its heightened consciousness, denies it any justice. Things finally come down to the business itself, to the act of revenge itself. The wretched mouse, in addition to the one original nastiness, has already managed to fence itself about with so many other nastinesses in the form of questions and doubts; it has padded out the one question with so many unresolved questions that, willy-nilly, some fatal slops have accumulated around it, some stinking filth consisting of its dubieties, anxieties, and, finally, of the spit raining on it from the ingenuous figures who stand solemnly around it like judges and dictators, guffawing at it from all their healthy gullets. Of course, nothing remains for it but to wave the whole thing aside with its little paw and, with a smile of feigned contempt, in which it does not believe itself, slip back shamefacedly into its crack. There, in its loathsome, stinking underground, our offended, beaten-down, and derided mouse at once immerses itself in cold, venomous, and, above all, everlasting spite. For forty years on end it will recall its offense to the last, most shameful details, each time adding even more shameful details of its own, spitefully taunting and chafing itself with its fantasies. It will be ashamed of its fantasies, but all the same it will recall everything, go over everything, heap all sorts of figments on itself, under the pretext that they, too, could have happened, and forgive nothing. It may even begin to take revenge, but somehow in snatches, with piddling things, from behind the stove, incognito, believing neither in its right to revenge itself nor in the success of its vengeance, and knowing beforehand that it will suffer a hundred times more from all its attempts at revenge than will the object of its vengeance, who will perhaps not even scratch at the bite. On its deathbed it will again recall everything, adding the interest accumulated over all that time, and . . . But it is precisely in this cold, loathsome half-despair, half-belief, in this conscious burying oneself alive from grief for forty years in the underground, in this assiduously produced and yet somewhat dubious hopelessness of one's position, in all this poison of unsatisfied desires penetrating inward, in all this fever of hesitations, of decisions taken forever, and repentances coming again a moment later, that the very sap of that strange pleasure I was talking about consists. It is so subtle, sometimes so elusive of consciousness, that people who are even the slightest bit narrow-minded, or who simply have strong nerves, will not understand a single trace of it. "Perhaps," you will add, grinning, "those who have never been slapped will also not understand"—thereby politely hinting that I, too, may have experienced a slap in my life, and am therefore speaking as a connoisseur. I'll bet that's what you think. But calm yourselves, gentlemen, I have not received any slaps, though it's all quite the same to me whatever you may think about it. Perhaps I myself am sorry for having dealt out too few slaps in my life. But enough, not another word on this subject which you find so extremely interesting.

I calmly continue about people with strong nerves, who do not understand a certain refinement of pleasure. In the face of some mishaps, for example, these gentlemen may bellow at the top of their lungs like bulls, and let's suppose this brings them the greatest honor, but still, as I've already said, they instantly resign themselves before impossibility. Impossibility—meaning a stone wall? What stone wall? Well, of course, the laws of nature, the conclusions of natural science, mathematics. Once it's proved to you, for example, that you descended from an ape, there's no use making a wry face, just take it for what it is. Once it's proved to you that, essentially speaking, one little drop of your own fat should be dearer to you than a hundred thousand of your fellow men, and that in this result all so-called virtues and obligations and other ravings and prejudices will finally be resolved, go ahead and accept it, there's nothing to be done, because two times two is—mathematics. Try objecting to that.[5]

"For pity's sake," they'll shout at you, "you can't rebel: it's two times two is four! Nature doesn't ask your permission; it doesn't care about your wishes, or whether you like its laws or not. You're obliged to accept it as it is, and consequently all its results as well. And so a wall is indeed a wall . . . etc., etc." My God, but what do I care about the laws of nature and arithmetic if for some reason these laws and two times two is four are not to my liking? To be sure, I won't break through such a wall with my forehead if I really have not got strength enough to do it, but neither will I be reconciled with it simply because I have a stone wall here and have not got strength enough.

As if such a stone wall were truly soothing and truly contained in itself at least some word on the world, solely by being two times two is four. Oh, absurdity of absurdities! Quite another thing is to understand all, to be conscious of all, all impossibilities and stone walls; not to be reconciled with a single one of these impossibilities and stone walls if you are loath to be reconciled; to reach, by way of the most inevitable logical combinations, the most revolting conclusions on the eternal theme that you yourself seem somehow to blame even for the stone wall, though once again it is obviously clear that you are in no way to blame; and in consequence of that, silently and impotently gnashing your teeth, to come to a voluptuous standstill in inertia, fancying that, as it turns out, there isn't even anyone to be angry with; that there is no object to be found, and maybe never will be; that it's all a sleight-of-hand, a stacked deck, a cheat, that it's all just slops—nobody knows what and nobody knows who, but in spite of all the uncertainties and stacked decks, it still hurts, and the more uncertain you are, the more it hurts!

IV

"HA, HA, HA! Next you'll be finding pleasure in a toothache!" you will exclaim, laughing.

"And why not? There is also pleasure in a toothache," I will answer. I had a toothache for a whole month; I know there is. Here, of course, one does not remain silently angry, one moans; but these are not straightforward moans, they are crafty moans, and the craftiness is the whole point. These moans express the pleasure of the one who is suffering; if they did not give him pleasure, he wouldn't bother moaning. It's a good example, gentlemen, and I shall develop it. In these moans there is expressed, first, all the futility of our pain, so humiliating for our consciousness, and all the lawfulness of nature, on which, to be sure, you spit, but from which you suffer all the same, while it does not. There is expressed the consciousness that your enemy is nowhere to be found, and yet there is pain; the consciousness that, despite all possible Wagenheims,[6] you are wholly the slave of your teeth; that if someone wishes, your teeth will stop aching, and if not, they will go on aching for another three months; and that, finally, if you still do not agree, and protest even so, then the only consolation you have left is to whip yourself, or give your wall a painful beating with your fist, and decidedly nothing else. Well, sir, it is with these bloody offenses, with these mockeries from no one knows whom, that the pleasure finally begins, sometimes reaching the highest sensuality. I ask you, gentlemen: listen sometime to the moaning of an educated man of the nineteenth century who is suffering from a tooth-ache—say, on the second or third day of his ailment, when he's beginning to moan not as he did on the first day, that is, not simply because he has a toothache, not like some coarse peas-ant, but like a man touched by development and European civilization, like a man who has "renounced the soil and popu-lar roots," as they say nowadays.[7] His moans somehow turn bad, nastily wicked, and continue for whole days and nights. Yet he himself knows that his moans will be of no use to him; he knows better than anyone that he is only straining and irritating himself and others in vain; he knows that even the public before whom he is exerting himself, and his whole family, are already listening to him with loathing, do not believe even a pennyworth of it, and understand in them-selves that he could moan differently, more simply, without roulades and flourishes, and that it's just from spite and crafti-ness that he is playing around like that. Now, it is in all these consciousnesses and disgraces that the sensuality consists. "So I'm bothering you, straining your hearts, not letting anyone in the house sleep. Don't sleep, then; you, too, should feel every moment that I have a toothache. For you I'm no longer a hero, as I once wished to appear, but simply a vile little fel-low, a *chenapan*.[8] Well, so be it! I'm very glad you've gotten to the bottom of me. It's nasty for you listening to my mean little moans? Let it be nasty, then; here's an even nastier roulade for you . . ." You still don't understand, gentlemen? No, evidently one must attain a profundity of development and consciousness to understand all the curves of this sensual-

ity! You're laughing? I'm very glad. To be sure, gentlemen,
my jokes are in bad tone—uneven, confused, self-mistrustful.
But that is simply because I don't respect myself. How can a
man of consciousness have the slightest respect for himself?

V

No, HOW IS IT POSSIBLE, how is it at all possible for a
man to have the slightest respect for himself, if he has
presumed to find pleasure even in the very sense of his own
humiliation? I am not speaking this way now out of some
cloying repentance. And, generally, I hated saying: "Forgive
me, papa, I won't do it again"—not because I was incapable of
saying it, but, on the contrary, perhaps precisely because I
was all too capable of it. And how! As if on purpose, I used
to bumble into it on occasions when I'd never thought or
dreamed of doing anything wrong. That was the nastiest
thing of all. And there I'd be again, waxing tenderhearted,
repenting, shedding tears, and certainly hoodwinking myself,
though I wasn't pretending in the least. It was my heart that
somehow kept mucking things up . . . Here even the laws of
nature could no longer be blamed, though still, throughout
my life, the laws of nature have offended me constantly and
more than anything else. It's nasty to look back on it all, and
it was nasty then as well. For a minute or so later I'd be reasoning spitefully that it was all a lie, a lie, a loathsome, affected
lie—that is, all these repentances, tenderheartednesses, all these
vows of regeneration. And you ask why I twisted and tormented myself so? Answer: because it was just too boring
to sit there with folded arms, that's why I'd get into such
flourishes. Really, it was so. Observe yourselves more closely,
gentlemen, and you'll understand that it is so. I made up
adventures and devised a life for myself so as to live, at least

somehow, a little. How many times it happened to me—well, say, for example, to feel offended, just so, for no reason, on purpose; and I'd know very well that I felt offended for no reason, that I was affecting it, but you can drive yourself so far that in the end, really, you do indeed get offended. Somehow all my life I've had an urge to pull such stunts, so that in the end I could no longer control myself. Another time, twice even, I decided to force myself to fall in love. And I did suffer, gentlemen, I assure you. Deep in one's soul it's hard to believe one is suffering, mockery is stirring there, but all the same I suffer, and in a real, honest-to-god way; I get jealous, lose my temper . . . And all that from boredom, gentlemen, all from boredom; crushed by inertia. For the direct, lawful, immediate fruit of consciousness is inertia—that is, a conscious sitting with folded arms. I've already mentioned this above. I repeat, I emphatically repeat: ingenuous people and active figures are all active simply because they are dull and narrow-minded. How to explain it? Here's how: as a consequence of their narrow-mindedness, they take the most immediate and secondary causes for the primary ones, and thus become convinced more quickly and easily than others that they have found an indisputable basis for their doings, and so they feel at ease; and that, after all, is the main thing. For in order to begin to act, one must first be completely at ease, so that no more doubts remain. Well, and how am I, for example, to set myself at ease? Where are the primary causes on which I can rest, where are my bases? Where am I going to get them? I exercise thinking, and, consequently, for me every primary cause immediately drags with it yet another, still more primary one, and so on ad infinitum. Such is precisely the essence of all consciousness and thought. So, once again it's the laws of nature. And what, finally, is the result? The same old thing. Remember: I was speaking just now about revenge. (You probably didn't grasp it.) I said: a man takes revenge because he finds justice in it. That means he has found a primary cause, a basis—namely, justice. So he is set at ease on all sides and, consequently, takes his revenge calmly and successfully, being convinced that he is doing an honest and just thing. Whereas I do not see any justice here, nor do I find any virtue in it, and, consequently, if I set about taking revenge, it will be solely out of wickedness. Wickedness could, of course, overcome everything, all my doubts, and thus could serve quite successfully in place of a primary cause, precisely in that it is not a cause. But what's to be done if there is also no wickedness in me? (I did begin with that just now.) The spite in me, again as a consequence of those cursed laws of consciousness, undergoes a chemical breakdown. Before your eyes the object vanishes, the reasons evaporate, the culprit is not to be found, the offense becomes not an offense but a *fatum*, something like a toothache, for which no one is to blame, and, consequently, what remains is again the same way out—that is, to give the wall a painful beating. And so you just wave it aside, because you haven't found the primary cause. But try getting blindly carried away by your feelings, without reasoning, without a primary cause, driving consciousness away at least for a time; start hating, or fall in love, only so as not to sit with folded arms. The day after tomorrow, at the very latest, you'll begin to despise yourself for having knowingly hoodwinked yourself. The result: a soap bubble, and inertia. Oh, gentlemen, perhaps I really regard myself as an intelligent man only because throughout my entire life I've never been able to start or finish anything. Granted, granted I'm a babbler, a harmless, irksome babbler, as we all are. But what's to be done if the sole and express purpose of every intelligent man is babble—that is, a deliberate pouring from empty into void.

VI

O<small>H, IF</small> I <small>WERE</small> doing nothing only out of laziness. Lord, how I'd respect myself then. Respect myself precisely because I'd at least be capable of having laziness in me; there would be in me at least one, as it were, positive quality, which I myself could be sure of. Question: who is he? Answer: a lazybones. Now, it would be most agreeable to hear that about myself. It means I'm positively defined; it means there's something to say about me. "Lazybones!"—now, that is a title and a mission, it's a career, sirs. No joking, it really is. By rights I'm then a member of the foremost club, and my sole occupation is ceaselessly respecting myself. I knew a gentleman who prided himself all his life on being a fine judge of Lafite. He regarded it as his positive merit and never doubted himself. He died not merely with a serene but with a triumphant conscience, and he was perfectly right. And so I would choose a career for myself: I would be a lazybones and a glutton, and not just an ordinary one, but, for example, one sympathizing with everything beautiful and lofty. How do you like that? I've long been fancying it. This "beautiful and lofty" has indeed weighed heavy on my head in my forty years; but that's *my* forty years, while then—oh, then it would be different! I would at once find an appropriate activity for myself— namely, drinking the health of all that is beautiful and lofty. I would seize every occasion, first to shed a tear into my glass, and then to drink it for all that is beautiful and lofty. I would then turn everything in the world into the beautiful and lofty; in the vilest, most unquestionable trash I would discover the beautiful and lofty. I'd become as tearful as a sodden sponge. An artist, for example, has painted a Ge picture.[9] I immediately drink the health of the artist who has painted the Ge picture, because I love all that is beautiful and lofty. An author has written "*as anyone pleases*";[10] I immediately drink the health of "anyone who pleases," because I love all that is "beautiful and lofty." For this I'll demand to be respected, I'll persecute whoever does not show me respect. I live peacefully, I die solemnly—why, this is charming, utterly charming! And I'd grow myself such a belly then, I'd fashion such a triple chin for myself, I'd fix myself up such a ruby nose that whoever came along would say, looking at me: "Now, there's a plus! There's a real positive!" And, think what you will, it's most agreeable to hear such comments in our negative age, gentlemen.

VII

BUT THESE ARE ALL golden dreams. Oh, tell me, who first announced, who was the first to proclaim that man does dirty only because he doesn't know his real interests; and that were he to be enlightened, were his eyes to be opened to his real, normal interests, man would immediately stop doing dirty, would immediately become good and noble, because, being enlightened and understanding his real profit, he would see his real profit precisely in the good, and it's common knowledge that no man can act knowingly against his own profit, consequently, out of necessity, so to speak, he would start doing good? Oh, the babe! oh, the pure, innocent child! and when was it, to begin with, in all these thousands of years, that man acted solely for his own profit? What is to be done with the millions of facts testifying to how people *knowingly*, that is, fully understanding their real profit, would put it in second place and throw themselves onto another path, a risk, a perchance, not compelled by anyone or anything, but precisely as if they simply did not want the designated path, and stubbornly, willfully pushed off onto another one, difficult, absurd, searching for it all but in the dark. So, then, this stubbornness and willfulness were really more agreeable to them than any profit ... Profit! What is profit? And will you take it upon yourself to define with perfect exactitude precisely what man's profit consists in? And what if it so happens that *on occasion* man's profit not only may but precisely must consist in sometimes wishing what is bad for himself, and not what is profitable? And if so, if there can be such a case, then the whole rule goes up in smoke. What do you think, can such a case occur? You're laughing; laugh then, gentlemen, only answer me: has man's profit been calculated quite correctly? Isn't there something that not only has not been but even cannot be fitted into any classification? Because, gentlemen, as far as I know, you have taken your whole inventory of human profits from an average of statistical figures and scientifico-economic formulas. Because profit for you is prosperity, wealth, freedom, peace, and so on and so forth; so that a man who, for example, openly and knowingly went against this whole inventory would, in your opinion—well, and also in mine, of course—be an obscurantist or a complete madman, right? But here is the surprising thing: how does it happen that all these statisticians, sages, and lovers of mankind, in calculating human profits, constantly omit one profit? They don't even take it into account in the way it ought to be taken, and yet the whole account depends on that. It's no great trouble just to take it, this profit, and include it in the list. But that's the whole bane of it, that this tricky profit doesn't fall into any classification, doesn't fit into any list. I, for instance, have a friend ... Eh, gentlemen! but he's your friend as well; and whose friend is he not! Preparing to do something, this gentleman will at once expound to you, with great eloquence and clarity, precisely how he must needs act in accordance with the laws of reason and truth. Moreover: with passion and excitement he will talk to you of real, normal human interests; with mockery he will reproach those shortsighted fools who understand neither their own profit nor the true meaning of virtue; and then, exactly a quarter of an hour later, without any sudden, extraneous cause, but precisely because of something within him that is stronger than all his interests, he'll cut quite a different caper, that is, go obviously against what he himself was just saying: against the laws of reason, against his own profit; well, in short, against everything . . . I warn you that my friend is a collective person, and therefore it is somehow difficult to blame him alone. That's just the thing, gentlemen, that there may well exist something that is dearer for almost every man than his very best profit, or (so as not to violate logic) that there is this one most profitable profit (precisely the omitted one, the one we were just talking about), which is chiefer and more profitable than all other profits, and for which a man is ready, if need be, to go against all laws, that is, against reason, honor, peace, prosperity—in short, against all these beautiful and useful things—only so as to attain this primary, most profitable profit which is dearer to him than anything else.

"Well, but it is a profit, after all," you will interrupt me. I beg your pardon, sirs, but we shall speak further of it, and the point is not in a play on words, but in the fact that this profit is remarkable precisely because it destroys all our classifications and constantly shatters all the systems elaborated by lovers of mankind for the happiness of mankind. Interferes with everything, in short. But before naming this profit for you, I want to compromise myself personally, and therefore I boldly declare that all these beautiful systems, all these theories that explain to mankind its true, normal interests, so that, striving necessarily to attain these interests, it would at once become good and noble—all this, in my opinion, is so far only logistics! Yes, sirs, logistics! For merely to assert this theory of the renewal of all mankind by means of a system of its own profits—this, to my mind, is almost the same as . . . well, let's say, for example, the same as asserting, with Buckle, that man gets softer from civilization and, consequently, becomes less bloodthirsty and less capable of war.[11] Logically, it seems, that's what he comes up with. But man is so partial to systems and abstract conclusions that he is ready intentionally to distort the truth, to turn a blind eye and a deaf ear, only so as to justify his logic. That's why I've chosen this example, because it is an all too vivid one. Why, look around you: blood is flowing in rivers, and in such a jolly way besides, like champagne. Take this whole nineteenth century of ours, in which Buckle also lived. Take Napoleon—both the great one and the present one. Take North America—that everlasting union. Take, finally, this caricature of a Schleswig-Holstein . . .[12] What is it that civilization softens in us? Civilization cultivates only a versatility of sensations in man, and . . . decidedly nothing else. And through the development of this versatility, man may even reach the point of finding pleasure in blood. Indeed, this has already happened to him. Have you noticed that the most refined blood-shedders have almost all been the most civilized gentlemen, to whom the various Attilas and Stenka Razins[13] sometimes could not hold a candle? And if they don't strike one as sharply as Attila or Stenka Razin, it is precisely because they occur too frequently, they are too ordinary, too familiar a sight. If man has not become more bloodthirsty from civilization, at any rate he has certainly become bloodthirsty in a worse, a viler way than formerly. Formerly, he saw justice in bloodshed and with a quiet conscience exterminated whoever he had to; while now, though we do regard bloodshed as vile, we still occupy ourselves with this vileness, and even more than formerly. Which is worse?—decide for yourselves. They say that Cleopatra (excuse this example from Roman history) liked to stick golden pins into her slave girls' breasts, and took pleasure in their screaming and writhing. You'll say that this was, relatively speaking, in barbarous times; that now, too, the times are barbarous because (again relatively speaking) now, too, pins get stuck in; that now, too, though man has learned to see more clearly on occasion than in barbarous times, he is still far from *having grown accustomed* to acting as reason and science dictate. But even so you are perfectly confident that he will not fail to grow accustomed once one or two old bad habits have passed and once common sense and science have thoroughly re-educated and given a normal direction to human nature. You are confident that man will then *voluntarily* cease making mistakes and, willy-nilly, so to speak, refuse to set his will at variance with his normal interests. Moreover: then, you say, science itself will teach man (though this is really a luxury in my opinion) that in fact he has neither will nor caprice, and never did have any, and that he himself is nothing but a sort of piano key or a sprig in an organ;[14] and that, furthermore, there also exist in the world the laws of nature; so that whatever he does is done not at all according to his own wanting, but of itself, according to the laws of nature. Consequently, these laws of nature need only be discovered, and then man will no longer be answerable for his actions, and his life will become extremely easy. Needless to say, all human actions will then be calculated according to these laws, mathematically, like a table of logarithms, up to 108,000, and entered into a calendar; or, better still, some well-meaning publications will appear, like the present-day encyclopedic dictionaries, in which everything will be so precisely calculated and designated that there will no longer be any actions or adventures in the world.

And it is then—this is still you speaking—that new economic relations will come, quite ready-made, and also calculated with mathematical precision, so that all possible questions will vanish in an instant, essentially because they will have been given all possible answers. Then the crystal palace will get built.[15] Then ... well, in short, then the bird Kagan will come flying.[16] Of course, there's no guaranteeing (this is me speaking now) that it won't, for example, be terribly boring then (because what is there to do if everything's calculated according to some little table?), but, on the other hand, it will all be extremely reasonable. Of course, what inventions can boredom not lead to! Golden pins also get stuck in from boredom, but all that would be nothing. The bad thing is (this is me speaking again) that, for all I know, they may be glad of the golden pins then. Man really is stupid, phenomenally stupid. That is, he's by no means stupid, but rather he's so ungrateful that it would be hard to find the likes of him. I, for example, would not be the least bit surprised if suddenly, out of the blue, amid the universal future reasonableness, some gentleman of ignoble, or, better, of retrograde and jeering physiognomy, should emerge, set his arms akimbo, and say to us all: "Well, gentlemen, why don't we reduce all this reasonableness to dust with one good kick, for the sole purpose of sending all these logarithms to the devil and living once more according to our own stupid will!" That would still be nothing, but what is offensive is that he'd be sure to find followers: that's how man is arranged. And all this for the emptiest of reasons, which would seem not even worth mentioning: namely, that man, whoever he might be, has always and everywhere liked to act as he wants, and not at all as reason and profit dictate; and one can want even against one's own profit, and one sometimes even *positively must* (this is my idea now). One's own free and voluntary wanting, one's own caprice, however wild, one's own fancy, though chafed sometimes to the point of madness—all this is that same most profitable profit, the omitted one, which does not fit into any classification, and because of which all systems and theories are constantly blown to the devil. And where did all these sages get the idea that man needs some normal, some virtuous wanting? What made them necessarily imagine that what man needs is necessarily a reasonably profitable wanting? Man needs only *independent* wanting, whatever this independence may cost and wherever it may lead. Well, and this wanting, the devil knows . . .

VIII

"HA, HA, HA! but in fact, if you want to know, there isn't any wanting!" you interrupt with a guffaw. "Today's science has even so succeeded in anatomizing man up that we now know that wanting and so-called free will are nothing else but . . ."

Wait, gentlemen, I myself wanted to begin that way. I confess, I even got scared. I just wanted to cry out that wanting depends on the devil knows what, and thank God, perhaps, for that, but I remembered about this science and . . . backed off. And just then you started talking. And indeed, well, if one day they really find the formula for all our wantings and caprices—that is, what they depend on, by precisely what laws they occur, precisely how they spread, what they strive for in such-and-such a case, and so on and so forth; a real, mathematical formula, that is—then perhaps man will immediately stop wanting; what's more, perhaps he will certainly stop. Who wants to want according to a little table? Moreover: he will immediately turn from a man into a sprig in an organ or something of the sort; because what is man without desires, without will, and without wantings, if not a sprig in an organ barrel? What do you think?—let's reckon up the probabilities—can it happen or not?

"Hm . . ." you decide, "our wantings are for the most part mistaken owing to a mistaken view of our profit. We sometimes want pure rubbish precisely because, in our stupidity, we see this rubbish as the easiest path to the attainment of some preconceived profit. Well, but when it's all explained, worked out on a piece of paper (which is quite possible because, after all, it's vile and senseless to believe beforehand that there are certain laws of nature which man will never learn)—then, to be sure, there will be no more so-called desires. For if wanting someday gets completely in cahoots with reason, then essentially we shall be reasoning and not wanting, because it really is impossible, for example, while preserving reason, to *want* senselessness and thus knowingly go against reason and wish yourself harm ... And since all wantings and reasonings can indeed be calculated—because, after all, they will someday discover the laws of our so-called free will—then consequently, and joking aside, something like a little table can be arranged, so that we shall indeed want according to this little table. For if it should someday be worked out and proved to me that when I made a fig at such-and-such a person, it was precisely because I could not do otherwise, and that I was bound to do it with such-and-such a finger, then what is left so *free* in me, especially if I am a learned man and have completed a course of studies somewhere? No, then I can calculate my life for thirty years ahead; in short, if this does get arranged, then we really will have no choice; we'll have to accept it in any case. And, generally, we ought tirelessly to repeat to ourselves that, precisely at such-and-such a moment, in such-and-such circumstances, nature does not ask our permission; that it must be accepted as it is, and not as we fancy, and if we are really aiming at a little table and a calendar, and ... well, and even at a retort, then there's no help for it, we must accept the retort! Or else it will get accepted of itself, without you ..."

Yes, sirs, but for me that's just where the hitch comes! You will forgive me, gentlemen, for philosophizing away; it's a matter of forty years underground! Allow me to indulge my fancy a bit. You see: reason, gentlemen, is a fine thing, that is unquestionable, but reason is only reason and satisfies only man's reasoning capacity, while wanting is a manifestation of the whole of life—that is, the whole of human life, including reason and various little itches. And though our life in this manifestation often turns out to be a bit of trash, still it is life and not just the extraction of a square root. I, for example, quite naturally want to live so as to satisfy my whole capacity for living, and not so as to satisfy just my reasoning capacity alone, which is some twentieth part of my whole capacity for living. What does reason know? Reason knows only what it has managed to learn (some things, perhaps, it will never learn; this is no consolation, but why not say it anyway?), while human nature acts as an entire whole, with everything that is in it, consciously and unconsciously, and though it lies, still it lives. I suspect, gentlemen, that you are looking at me with pity; you repeat to me that an enlightened and developed man, such, in short, as the future man will be, simply cannot knowingly want anything unprofitable for himself, that this is mathematics. I agree completely, it is indeed mathematics. But I repeat to you for the hundredth time, there is only one case, one only, when man may purposely, consciously wish for himself even the harmful, the stupid, even what is stupidest of all: namely, so as *to have the right* to wish for himself even what is stupidest of all and not be bound by an obligation to wish for himself only what is intelligent. For this stupidest of all, this caprice of ours, gentlemen, may in fact be the most profitable of anything on earth for our sort, especially in certain cases. And in particular it may be more profitable than all other profits even in the case when it is obviously harmful and contradicts the most sensible conclusions of our reason concerning profits—because in any event it preserves for us the chiefest and dearest thing, that is, our personality and our individuality. Now, some insist that this is indeed the dearest of all things for man; wanting may, of course, converge with reason, if it wants, especially if this is not abused but is done with moderation; it is both useful and sometimes even praiseworthy. But wanting is very often, and even for the most part, completely and stubbornly at odds with reason, and . . . and . . . and, do you know, this, too, is useful and sometimes even quite praiseworthy? Suppose, gentlemen, that man is not stupid. (Really, it is quite impossible to say he is, for the sole reason that if he is stupid, who then is intelligent?) But even if he isn't stupid, all the same he's monstrously ungrateful! Phenomenally ungrateful. I even think the best definition of man is: a being that goes on two legs and is ungrateful. But that's still not all; that's still not his chief defect; his chiefest defect is his constant lack of good behavior—constant from the great flood to the Schleswig-Holstein period of man's destiny. Lack of good behavior and, consequently, lack of good sense; for it has long been known that lack of good sense comes from nothing else but the lack of good behavior. Try casting a glance at the history of mankind; well, what will you see? Majestic? Maybe it is majestic; the Colossus of Rhodes alone, for example, is worth something! Not without reason did Mr. Anaevsky[17] testify that while some say it was the work of human hands, others insist it was created by nature itself. Colorful? Maybe it is colorful; one need only sort through the full-dress military and civil uniforms of all times and all peoples—that alone is worth something, and if you were to add the uniforms of the lower civil ranks, you could really break a leg; no historian would be left standing. Monotonous? Well, maybe also monotonous: they fight and fight, they fight now, and fought before, and fought afterwards—you'll agree it's even all too monotonous. In short, anything can be said about world history, anything that might just enter the head of the most disturbed imagination. Only one thing cannot be said—that it is sensible. You'd choke on the first word. And one even comes upon this sort of thing all the time: there constantly appear in life people of such good behavior and good sense, such sages and lovers of mankind, as precisely make it their goal to spend their entire lives in the best-behaved and most sensible way possible, to become, so to speak, a light for their neighbors, essentially in order to prove to them that one can indeed live in the world as a person of good behavior and good sense. And what then? It is known that sooner or later, towards the end of their lives, many of these lovers have betrayed themselves, producing some anecdote, sometimes even of the most indecent sort. Now I ask you: what can be expected of man as a being endowed with such strange qualities? Shower him with all earthly blessings, drown him in happiness completely, over his head, so that only bubbles pop up on the surface of happiness, as on water; give him such economic satisfaction that he no longer has anything left to do at all except sleep, eat gingerbread, and worry about the noncessation of world history—and it is here, just here, that he, this man, out of sheer ingratitude, out of sheer lampoonery, will do something nasty. He will even risk his gingerbread, and wish on purpose for the most pernicious nonsense, the most noneconomical meaninglessness, solely in order to mix into all this positive good sense his own pernicious, fantastical element. It is precisely his fantastic dreams, his most banal stupidity, that he will wish to keep hold of, with the sole purpose of confirming to himself (as if it were so very necessary) that human beings are still human beings and not piano keys, which, though played upon with their own hands by the laws of nature themselves, are in danger of being played so much that outside the calendar it will be impossible to want anything. And more than that: even if it should indeed turn out that he is a piano key, if it were even proved to him mathematically and by natural science, he would still not come to reason, but would do something contrary on purpose, solely out of ingratitude alone; essentially to have his own way. And if he finds himself without means—he will invent destruction and chaos, he will invent all kinds of suffering, and still have his own way! He will launch a curse upon the world, and since man alone is able to curse (that being his privilege, which chiefly distinguishes him from other animals), he may achieve his end by the curse alone—that is, indeed satisfy himself that he is a man and not a piano key! If you say that all this, the chaos and darkness and cursing, can also be calculated according to a little table, so that the mere possibility of a prior calculation will put a stop to it all and reason will claim its own—then he will deliberately go mad for the occasion, so as to do without reason and still have his own way! I believe in this, I will answer for this, because the whole human enterprise seems indeed to consist in man's proving to himself every moment that he is a man and not a sprig! With his own skin if need be, but proving it; by troglodytism if need be, but proving it. And how not sin after that, how not boast that this has still not come about, and that wanting so far still depends on the devil knows what . . .

You shout at me (if you do still honor me with your shouts) that no one is taking my will from me here; that all they're doing here is busily arranging it somehow so that my will, of its own will, coincides with my normal interests, with the laws of nature, and with arithmetic.

Eh, gentlemen, what sort of will of one's own can there be if it comes to tables and arithmetic, and the only thing going is two times two is four? Two times two will be four even without my will. As if that were any will of one's own!

IX

GENTLEMEN, I am joking, of course, and I myself know that I am not joking very successfully, but one really cannot take everything as a joke. Maybe I'm grinding my teeth as I joke. Gentlemen, I am tormented by questions; resolve them for me. You, for example, want to make man unlearn his old habits, and to correct his will in conformity with the demands of science and common sense. But how do you know that man not only can be but *must* be remade in this way? What makes you conclude that man's wanting so necessarily *needs* to be corrected? In short, how do you know that such a correction will indeed be profitable for man? And, if we're to say everything, why are you so *certainly* convinced that not to go against real, normal profits, guaranteed by the arguments of reason and arithmetic, is indeed always profitable for man and is a law for the whole of mankind? So far, it's still just your supposition. Suppose it is a law of logic, but perhaps not of mankind at all. Perhaps you think, gentlemen, that I am mad? Allow me an observation. I agree: man is predominantly a creating animal, doomed to strive consciously towards a goal and to occupy himself with the art of engineering—that is, to eternally and ceaselessly make a road for himself that at least goes *somewhere or other*. But sometimes he may wish to swerve aside, precisely because he is *doomed* to open this road, and also perhaps because, stupid though the ingenuous figure generally is, it still sometimes occurs to him that this road almost always turns out to go *somewhere or other*, and the main thing is not where it goes, but that it should simply be going, and that the well-behaved child, by neglecting the art of engineering, not give himself up to pernicious idleness, which, as is known, is the mother of all vice. Man loves creating and the making of roads, that is indisputable. But why does he so passionately love destruction and chaos as well? Tell me that! But of this I wish specially to say a couple of words myself. Can it be that he has such a love of destruction and chaos (it's indisputable that he sometimes loves them very much; that is a fact) because he is instinctively afraid of achieving the goal and completing the edifice he is creating? How do you know, maybe he likes the edifice only from far off, and by no means up close; maybe he only likes creating it, and not living in it, leaving it afterwards *aux animaux domestiques*,[18] such as ants, sheep, and so on and so forth. Now, ants have totally different tastes. They have a remarkable edifice of the same sort, forever indestructible—the anthill.

With the anthill the most reverend ants began, and with the anthill they will doubtless end as well, which does great credit to their constancy and positiveness. But man is a frivolous and unseemly being, and perhaps, similar to a chess player, likes only the process of achieving the goal, but not the goal itself. And who knows (one cannot vouch for it), perhaps the whole goal mankind strives for on earth consists just in this ceaselessness of the process of achievement alone, that is to say, in life itself, and not essentially in the goal, which, of course, is bound to be nothing other than two times two is four—that is, a formula; and two times two is four is no longer life, gentlemen, but the beginning of death. At least man has always somehow feared this two times two is four, and I fear it even now. Suppose all man ever does is search for this two times two is four; he crosses oceans, he sacrifices his life in the search; but to search it out, actually to find it—by God, he's somehow afraid. For he senses that once he finds it, there will be nothing to search for. Workers, when they're done work-

ing, at least get their pay, go to a pot-house, then wind up with
the police—so it keeps them busy for a week. But where is
man to go? Something awkward, at any rate, can be noticed
in him each time he achieves some such goal. Achieving he
likes, but having achieved he does not quite like, and that, of
course, is terribly funny. In short, man is comically arranged;
there is apparently a joke in all this. But still, two times two is
four is a most obnoxious thing. Two times two is four—why,
in my opinion, it's sheer impudence, sirs. Two times two is
four has a cocky look; it stands across your path, arms akimbo,
and spits. I agree that two times two is four is an excellent
thing; but if we're going to start praising everything, then
two times two is five is sometimes also a most charming little
thing.

And why are you so firmly, so solemnly convinced that
only the normal and the positive, in short, that only well-
being, is profitable for man? Is reason not perhaps mistaken
as to profits? Maybe man does not love well-being only?
Maybe he loves suffering just as much? Maybe suffering is
just as profitable for him as well-being? For man sometimes
loves suffering terribly much, to the point of passion, and that
is a fact. Here there's not even any need to consult world
history; just ask yourself, if you're a human being and have
had any life at all. As for my personal opinion, to love just
well-being alone is even somehow indecent. Whether it's
good or bad, it's sometimes also very pleasant to break something. I, as a matter of fact, take my stand here neither with
suffering nor with well-being. I stand . . . for my own caprice,
and that it be guaranteed me when necessary. Suffering, for
example, is inadmissible in vaudevilles, I know that. In a crystal palace it is even unthinkable: suffering is doubt, it is nega-
tion, and what good is a crystal palace in which one can have
doubts? And yet I'm certain that man will never renounce
real suffering, that is, destruction and chaos. Suffering—why,

this is the sole cause of consciousness. Though I did declare at the beginning that consciousness, in my opinion, is man's greatest misfortune, still I know that man loves it and will not exchange it for any satisfactions. Consciousness, for example, is infinitely higher than two times two. After two times two there would, of course, be nothing left—not only to do, but even to learn. The only possible thing to do then would be to stop up our five senses and immerse ourselves in contemplation. Well, but with consciousness, though the result comes out the same—that is, again there's nothing to do—at least one can occasionally whip oneself, and, after all, that livens things up a bit. It may be retrograde, but still it's better than nothing.

X

YOU BELIEVE in a crystal edifice, forever indestructible; that is, in an edifice at which one can neither put out one's tongue on the sly nor make a fig in the pocket.[19] Well, and perhaps I'm afraid of this edifice precisely because it is crystal and forever indestructible, and it will be impossible to put out one's tongue at it even on the sly.

Now look: if instead of a palace there is a chicken coop, and it starts to rain, I will perhaps get into the chicken coop to avoid a wetting, but all the same I will not take the chicken coop for a palace out of gratitude for its having kept me from the rain. You laugh, you even say that in that case it makes no difference—chicken coop or mansion. Yes, say I, if one were to live only so as not to get wet.

But what's to be done if I've taken it into my head that one does not live only for that, and that if one is to live, it had better be in a mansion? This is my wanting, this is my desire. You will scrape it out of me only when you change my desires. So, change them, seduce me with something else, give

me a different ideal. But meanwhile I will not take a chicken
coop for a palace. Let it even be so that the crystal edifice is a
bluff, that by the laws of nature it should not even be, and
that I've invented it only as a result of my own stupidity, as
a result of certain old nonrational habits of our generation.
But what do I care if it should not be? What difference does
it make, since it exists in my desires, or, better, exists as long
as my desires exist? Perhaps you're laughing again? Laugh,
if you please; I will accept all mockery, but still I won't say
I'm full when I'm hungry; still I know that I will not rest
with a compromise, with a ceaseless, recurring zero, simply
because according to the laws of nature it exists, and exists
really. I will not take a tenement house, with apartments for
the poor, and a thousand-year lease, and the dentist Wagenheim's shingle for good measure, as the crown of my desires.
Destroy my desires, wipe out my ideals, show me something
better, and I will follow you. Perhaps you'll say it's not worth
getting involved; but in that case I can answer you the same
way. Our discussion is serious; if you do not deign to give me
your attention, I am not going to bow and scrape before you.
I have the underground.

But so long as I live and desire—let my hand wither[20] if I
bring even one little brick for such a tenement house! Never
mind that I myself have just rejected the crystal edifice, for
the sole reason that one cannot taunt it with one's tongue. I
said that not because I have such a love of putting out my
tongue. Perhaps I was angry simply because such an edifice,
at which it is possible not to put out one's tongue, has never
yet been found among all your edifices. On the contrary, I
would let my tongue be cut off altogether, from sheer gratitude, if only it could be so arranged that I myself never felt
like sticking it out again. What do I care that it's impossible
to arrange it so, and one must content oneself with apart-

ments? Why, then, have I been arranged with such desires? Can it be that I've been arranged simply so as to come to the conclusion that my entire arrangement is a hoax? Can that be the whole purpose? I don't believe it.

You know what, though: I'm convinced that our sort, the underground ones, ought to be kept on a tether. Though we're capable of sitting silently in the underground for forty years, once we do come out and let loose, we talk, talk, talk ...

XI

THE FINAL END, gentlemen: better to do nothing! Better conscious inertia! And so, long live the underground! Though I did say that I envy the normal man to the point of uttermost bile, still I do not want to be him on those conditions in which I see him (though, all the same, I shall not stop envying him. No, no, the underground is in any case more profitable!). There one can at least ... Eh! but here, too, I'm lying! Lying, because I myself know, like two times two, that it is not at all the underground that is better, but something different, completely different, which I thirst for but cannot ever find! Devil take the underground!

Even this would be better here: if I myself believed at least something of all I've just written. For I swear to you, gentlemen, that I do not believe a word, not one little word, of all I've just scribbled! That is, I do believe, perhaps, but at the same time, who knows why, I sense and suspect that I'm lying like a cobbler.

"Then why did you write it all?" you say to me.

And what if I put you away for some forty years with nothing to do, and then come to you in the underground after forty years to see how you've turned out? One cannot leave a man alone and unoccupied for forty years, can one?

"But is this not shameful, is it not humiliating!" you will perhaps say to me, contemptuously shaking your heads. "You thirst for life, yet you yourself resolve life's questions with a logical tangle. And how importunate, how impudent your escapades, yet at the same time how frightened you are! You talk nonsense, and are pleased with it; you say impudent things, yet you keep being afraid and asking forgiveness for them. You insist that you are not afraid of anything, and at the same time you court our opinion. You insist that you are gnashing your teeth, and at the same time you exert your wit to make us laugh. You know that your witticisms are not witty, but you are apparently quite pleased with their literary merits. You may indeed have happened to suffer, but you do not have the least respect for your suffering. There is truth in you, too, but no integrity; out of the pettiest vanity you take your truth and display it, disgrace it, in the market-place . . . You do indeed want to say something, but you conceal your final word out of fear, because you lack the resolve to speak it out, you have only cowardly insolence. You boast about consciousness, yet all you do is vacillate, because, though your mind works, your heart is darkened by depravity, and without a pure heart there can be no full, right consciousness. And how importunate you are, how you foist yourself, how you mug! Lies, lies, lies!"

To be sure, I myself have just made up all these words of yours. This, too, is from underground. I've spent forty years on end there listening to these words of yours through a crack. I thought them up myself, since this was all that would get thought up. No wonder they got learned by heart and assumed a literary form . . .

But can it be, can it be that you are indeed so gullible as to imagine I will publish all this and, what's more, give it to you to read? And here's another puzzle for me: why indeed do I call you "gentlemen," why do I address you as if you were actually my readers? Such confessions as I intend to begin setting forth here are not published and given to others to read. At least I do not have so much firmness in myself, and do not consider it necessary to have it. But you see: a certain fancy has come into my head, and I want at all costs to realize it. Here's what it is.

In every man's memories there are such things as he will reveal not to everyone, but perhaps only to friends. There are also such as he will reveal not even to friends, but only to himself, and that in secret. Then, finally, there are such as a man is afraid to reveal even to himself, and every decent man will have accumulated quite a few things of this sort. That is, one might even say: the more decent a man is, the more of them he will have. At least I myself have only recently resolved to recall some of my former adventures, which till now I have always avoided, even with a certain uneasiness. Now, however, when I not only recall them but am even resolved to write them down, now I want precisely to make a test: is it possible to be perfectly candid with oneself and not be afraid of the whole truth? I will observe incidentally: Heine insists that faithful autobiographies are almost impossible, and that a man is sure to tell a pack of lies about himself. In his opinion, Rousseau, for example, most certainly told a pack of lies about himself in his confessions, and even did so intentionally, out of vanity.[21] I'm sure Heine is right; I understand very well how one can sometimes slap whole crimes on oneself solely out of vanity, and I even perceive quite well what sort of vanity it might be. But Heine's opinion concerned a man who was confessing before the public. I, however, am writing only for myself, and I declare once and for all that even if I write as if I were addressing readers, that is merely a front, because it's easier for me to write that way. It's a form, just an empty form, and I shall never have any readers. I have already declared as much . . .

I do not want to hamper myself with anything in preparing my notes. I will not introduce any order or system. Whatever I recall, I will write down.

Now, for example, someone might seize upon a word and ask me: if you really are not counting on any readers, why then do you make such agreements with yourself, and on paper besides, that you will introduce no order or system, that you will write down whatever you recall, etc., etc.? Why these explanations? Why these apologies?

"Well, so it goes," I reply.

There is, however, a whole psychology here. Maybe it's also that I'm simply a coward. And maybe also that I'm purposely imagining a public before me so as to behave more decently while I write. There may be a thousand reasons.

But here is another thing: for what and to what end, in fact, do I want to write? If not for the public, then why not simply recall everything mentally, without transferring it to paper?

Right, sir; but on paper it will somehow come out more solemnly. There's something imposing in it, there will be more of a judgment on oneself, it will gain in style. Besides: maybe I will indeed get relief from the writing. Today, for example, I'm particularly oppressed by one distant recollection. I recalled it clearly the other day, and it has since stayed with me like a nagging musical tune that refuses to be gotten rid of. And yet one must get rid of it. I have hundreds of such recollections; but some one out of a hundred emerges every now and then and oppresses me. I believe for some reason that if I write it down, I shall then be rid of it. So why not try?

Finally: I'm bored, and I constantly do nothing. And writing things down really seems like work. They say work makes a man good and honest. Well, here's a chance, at least.

Snow is falling today, almost wet, yellow, dull. And it was falling yesterday, and it was falling the other day as well. I think it was apropos of the wet snow that I recalled this anecdote that now refuses to be gotten rid of. And so, let this be a story apropos of the wet snow.[22]

II

Apropos of the Wet Snow

When from out of error's darkness
With a word both sure and ardent
I had drawn the fallen soul,
And you, filled with deepest torment,
Cursed the vice that had ensnared you
And so doing wrung your hands;
When, punishing with recollection
Forgetful conscience, you then told
The tale of all that went before me,
And suddenly you hid your face
In trembling hands and, filled with horror,
Filled with shame, dissolved in tears,
Indignant as you were, and shaken . . .
Etc., etc., etc.

From the poetry of N. A. Nekrasov[1]

I

AT THAT TIME I was only twenty-four years old. My life then was already gloomy, disorderly, and solitary to the point of savagery. I did not associate with anyone, even avoided speaking, and shrank more and more into my corner. At work, in the office, I even tried not to look at anyone, and

I noticed very well that my colleagues not only considered me an odd man, but—as I also kept fancying—seemed to look at me with a certain loathing. It used to occur to me: why does no one except me fancy that people look at him with loathing? There was one in our office who had a disgusting and most pockmarked face, even somehow like a bandit's. With such an indecent face, I think I wouldn't even have dared to glance at anyone. Another hadn't changed his uniform for so long that there was a bad smell in his vicinity. And yet neither of these gentlemen was embarrassed—either with regard to his clothes or his face, or somehow morally. Neither the one nor the other imagined that he was looked at with loathing; and even if they had imagined it, it would have been all the same to them, so long as their superiors did not deign to pay heed. It's perfectly clear to me now that it was I who, owing to my boundless vanity, and hence also my exactingness towards myself, very often looked upon myself with furious dissatisfaction, reaching the point of loathing, and therefore mentally attributed my view to everyone else. I hated my face, for example, found it odious, and even suspected that there was some mean expression in it, and therefore every time I came to work I made a painful effort to carry myself as independently as possible, so as not to be suspected of meanness, and to express as much nobility as possible with my face. "Let it not be a beautiful face," I thought, "but, to make up for that, let it be a noble, an expressive, and, above all, an *extremely* intelligent one." Yet I knew, with certainty and suffering, that I would never be able to express all those perfections with the face I had. The most terrible thing was that I found it positively stupid. And I would have been quite satisfied with intelligence. Let's even say I would even have agreed to a mean expression, provided only that at the same time my face be found terribly intelligent.

Of course, I hated them all in our office, from first to last, and despised them all, but at the same time I was also as if afraid of them. It happened that I would suddenly set them above myself. Things were somehow sudden with me in those days: now I despised them, now I set them above me. A developed and decent man cannot be vain without a boundless exactingness towards himself and without despising himself at moments to the point of hatred. But whether I despised them or set them above me, I used to drop my eyes before almost everyone I met. I even made experiments: will I be able to endure so-and-so's glance on me?—and I was always the first to drop my eyes. This tormented me to the point of fury. I was also afraid to the point of illness of being ridiculous, and therefore slavishly worshiped routine in everything to do with externals; I loved falling into the common rut, and feared any eccentricity in myself with all my soul. But how could I hold out? I was morbidly developed, as a man of our time ought to be developed. And they were all dull-witted and as like one another as a flock of sheep. Perhaps to me alone in the whole office did it constantly seem that I was a coward and a slave; it seemed so to me precisely because I was developed. But it not only seemed, in fact it really was so: I was a coward and a slave. I say it without any embarrassment. Every decent man of our time is and must be a coward and a slave. That is his normal condition. I am deeply convinced of it. He's made that way, and arranged for it. And not in the present time, owing to some sort of chance circumstances, but generally in all times a decent man must be a coward and a slave. That is the natural law of all decent people on earth. If one of them does happen to get up a bit of pluck in something, let him not be eased or pleased by that: he'll still quail before something else. Such is the sole and everlasting outcome. Only asses and their mongrels show pluck, and even then only up to that certain wall. It's not worth paying any attention to them, because they mean precisely nothing.

One other circumstance tormented me then: namely, that no one else was like me, and I was like no one else. "I am one, and they are *all*," thought I, and—I'd fall to thinking.

Which shows what a young pup I still was.

Contraries also occurred. It was sometimes so disgusting to go to the office: it reached the point that I would often come home from work sick. Then suddenly, for no reason at all, comes a spell of skepticism and indifference (everything came in spells with me), and here I am laughing at my own intolerance and fastidiousness, reproaching myself with *romanticism*. One moment I don't even want to speak with anyone, and the next I go so far that I'm not only chatting away, but am even deciding to become close with them. All fastidiousness would suddenly disappear at once, for no reason at all. Who knows, maybe I never had any, maybe it was just an affectation, out of books? To this day I haven't resolved this question. Once I even became quite friendly with them, began visiting their homes, playing preference, drinking vodka, discussing promotions . . . But allow me a digression here.

We Russians, generally speaking, have never had any stupid, translunary German, and more especially French, romantics, who are not affected by anything; let the earth crumble under them, let the whole of France perish on the barricades—they are what they are, they won't change even for the sake of decency, and they'll go on singing their translunary songs till their dying day, so to speak, because they're fools. But we, in our Russian land, have no fools; that is a known fact; that's what makes us different from all those other German lands. Consequently, we have no translunary natures in a pure state. It was our "positive" publicists and critics of the time, hunting after Kostanzhoglos and Uncle Pyotr Ivanoviches,[2] and being foolish enough to take them for our ideal, who heaped it all on our romantics, holding them to be of the same translunary sort as in Germany or France. On the contrary, the

properties of our romantic are utterly and directly opposite
to those of the translunary European, and no little European
yardstick will fit here. (Do permit me the use of this word
"romantic"—a venerable word, respectable, worthy, and
familiar to all.) The properties of our romantic are to understand everything, *to see everything, and to see often incom-
parably more clearly than our very most positive minds do*;
not to be reconciled with anyone or anything, but at the same
time not to spurn anything; to get around everything, to yield
to everything, to be politic with everyone; never to lose sight
of the useful, practical goal (some nice little government
apartment, a little pension, a little decoration or two)—to
keep an eye on this goal through all enthusiasms and little
volumes of lyrical verses, and at the same time also to preserve "the beautiful and lofty" inviolate in himself till his
dying day, and incidentally to preserve himself quite successfully as well, somehow in cotton wool, like some little piece
of jewelry, if only, shall we say, for the benefit of that same
"beautiful and lofty." He's a broad man, our romantic, and
the foremost knave of all our knaves, I can assure you of
that . . . even from experience. Naturally, all this is so if the
romantic is intelligent. That is—what am I saying!—the romantic is always intelligent; I merely wished to observe that,
while we do happen to have had some fool romantics, that
doesn't count, for the sole reason that while still in the bloom
of life they regenerated definitively into Germans and, to
preserve their little piece of jewelry more comfortably, settled somewhere rather in Weimar or the Schwarzwald.[3] I,
for example, sincerely despised my service employment, and
if I didn't go around spitting, it was only out of necessity,
because I was sitting there getting money for it. The result
being—you will note—that I still didn't go around spitting.
Our romantic would sooner lose his mind (which, however,

happens very seldom) than start spitting, unless he's got his eye on some other career, and he will never be kicked out, except perhaps that he might be carted off to the madhouse as "the king of Spain,"[4] and that only if he loses his mind very much. But among us only the weaklings and towheads lose their minds. While the countless number of romantics go on to achieve considerable rank. Remarkable versatility! And what capacity for the very most contradictory feelings! I took comfort in that even then, and am of the same mind now. That is why we have so many "broad natures" who even with the ultimate fall never lose their ideal; and though they wouldn't lift a finger for their ideal, though they are inveterate bandits and thieves, all the same they respect their original ideal to the point of tears and are remarkably honest in their souls. Yes, sirs, only among us can the most inveterate scoundrel be perfectly and even loftily honest in his soul, while not ceasing in the least to be a scoundrel. Time and again, I repeat, such practical rogues come out of our romantics (I use the word "rogue" lovingly); they suddenly display such a sense of reality and such knowledge of the positive that the amazed authorities and public can only stand dumbfounded, clucking their tongues at them.

The versatility is indeed amazing, and God knows what it will turn and develop into in subsequent circumstances, and what it promises us for our times to come. It's not bad material, sirs! I don't say this out of any ridiculous or homebrewed patriotism. However, I'm sure you again think I'm laughing. Or, who knows, maybe contrariwise—that is, you're quite sure I really think so. In any event, gentlemen, I shall regard both your opinions as an honor and a special pleasure. And do forgive me my digression.

Of course, I could not sustain this friendliness with my colleagues; I'd spit in their eyes and, as a result of my still youthful inexperience, even stop greeting them, as if I'd cut them off. However, this happened to me only once. Generally, I was always alone.

At home, to begin with, I mainly used to read. I wished to stifle with external sensations all that was ceaselessly boiling up inside me. And among external sensations the only one possible for me was reading. Reading was, of course, a great help—it stirred, delighted, and tormented me. But at times it bored me terribly. I still wanted to move about, and so I'd suddenly sink into some murky, subterranean, vile debauch— not a great, but a measly little debauch. There were measly little passions in me, sharp, burning, because of my permanent, morbid irritability. I was given to hysterical outbursts, with tears and convulsions. Apart from reading I had nowhere to turn—that is, there was nothing I could then respect in my surroundings, nothing I would be drawn to. What's more, anguish kept boiling up; a hysterical thirst for contradictions, contrasts, would appear, and so I'd set out on debauchery. It is not at all to justify myself that I've been doing all this talk-ing ... But no! that's a lie! I precisely wanted to justify my-self. I make this little note for myself, gentlemen. I don't want to lie. I've given my word.

My debauchery I undertook solitarily, by night, covertly, fearfully, filthily, with a shame that would not abandon me at the most loathsome moments, and at such moments even went so far as a curse. I was then already bearing the under-ground in my soul. I was terribly afraid of somehow being seen, met, recognized. I used to frequent various rather murky places.

Once, passing at night by some wretched little tavern, I saw through the lighted window some gentlemen fighting with their cues around the billiard table and one of them being chucked out the window. At another time I would have been filled with loathing; but one of those moments suddenly came over me, and I envied this chucked-out gentleman, envied him so much that I even went into the tavern, into the billiard room: "Perhaps I, too, will have a fight," I thought, "and get chucked out the window myself."

I was not drunk, but what do you want of me—anguish can eat a man into such hysterics! But it came to nothing. I proved incapable even of jumping out the window and left without having had any fight.

From the very first I was brought up short there by a certain officer.

I was standing beside the billiard table, blocking the way unwittingly, and he wanted to pass; he took me by the shoulders and silently—with no warning or explanation—moved me from where I stood to another place, and then passed by as if without noticing. I could even have forgiven a beating, but I simply could not forgive his moving me and in the end just not noticing me.

Devil knows what I'd have given then for a real, more regular quarrel, more decent, more, so to speak, *literary*! I had been treated like a fly. This officer was a good six feet tall; and I am a short and skinny man. The quarrel, however, was up to me: all I had to do was protest a bit and, of course, I'd be chucked out the window. But I changed my mind and preferred . . . to efface myself spitefully.

I left the tavern confused and agitated, went straight home, and the next day continued my little debauch still more timidly, downtroddenly, and sadly than before, as if with a tear in my eye—yet I did continue it. Do not think, however, that I turned coward before the officer out of cowardice: in my soul I have never been a coward, though I constantly turned coward in reality, but—don't laugh too quickly, there's an explanation for that; rest assured, I have an explanation for everything.

Oh, if this officer had been one of those who would agree

to fight a duel! But no, he was precisely one of those gentlemen (alas, long since vanished) who preferred to set about it
with billiard cues, or, like Lieutenant Pirogov in Gogol[5]—by
means of the authorities. But they would not fight a duel, and
in any case would regard a duel with our sort, the pencil-
pushers, as indecent—and they generally regarded dueling as
something inconceivable, freethinking, French, while giving ample offense themselves, especially in cases of six-foot-
tallness.

I turned coward not from cowardice, but from the most
boundless vanity. I was afraid, not of six-foot-tallness, nor of
being badly beaten and chucked out the window; I really
would have had physical courage enough; what I lacked
was sufficient moral courage. I was afraid that none of those
present—from the insolent marker to the last putrid and
blackhead-covered clerk with a collar of lard who was hanging about there—would understand, and that they would all
deride me if I started protesting and talking to them in literary language. Because among us to this day it is impossible
to speak of a point of honor—that is, not honor, but a point
of honor (*point d'honneur*)—otherwise than in literary language. In ordinary language there is no mention of a "point
of honor." I was quite sure (what a sense of reality, despite
all romanticism!) that they would all simply burst with laughter, and the officer would beat me, not simply, that is, inoffen-
sively, but would certainly start kicking me with his knee,
driving me in this manner around the billiard table, and only
then perhaps have mercy and chuck me out the window.
Of course, for me this measly story could not end there.
Later I often met this officer in the street and made good note
of him. Only I don't know whether he recognized me. Probably not; I conclude that from certain signs. I, however, I—
looked at him with spite and hatred, and so it continued . . .
for several years, sirs! My spite even kept strengthening and

burgeoning with the years. First I quietly began finding things out about this officer. This was not easy for me, because I had no acquaintances. But once someone called him by his surname in the street while I was following him at a distance, as if tied to him, and so I learned his surname. Another time I trailed him all the way home, and for ten kopecks found out from the caretaker where he lived, on what floor, alone or with someone, and so on—in short, everything that can be learned from a caretaker. Then one morning, though I had never literaturized, it suddenly came into my head to describe this officer in the manner of an esposé, as a caricature, in a story. It was a delight to me to write this story. I esposed him, even slandered him a bit; at first I distorted his surname in a way that made it immediately recognizable, but then, on riper reflection, I changed it and sent the story to *Fatherland Notes*. But there were no esposés yet, and my story wasn't published.[6] I found this quite vexing. There were times when I was simply choking with spite. In the end I decided to challenge my adversary to a duel. I composed a beautiful, attractive letter to him, entreating him to apologize to me; and hinted quite strongly at a duel in case of refusal. The letter was composed in such a way that if the officer had even the slightest notion of "the beautiful and lofty," he could not fail to come running to me, to throw himself on my neck and offer me his friendship. And that would be so nice! What a life we would have, what a life! He would protect me with his dignity; I would ennoble him with my development and, well . . . ideas, and there could be so much of this or that! Imagine, by then it was already two years since he had offended me, and my challenge was a most outrageous anachronism, in spite of all the cleverness of my letter in explaining away and concealing the anachronism. But, thank God (to this day I thank the Almighty with tears), I did not send my letter. I go cold all over when I recall what might have happened if I had sent it. And suddenly . . . suddenly I got my revenge in the simplest, the most brilliant way! The brightest idea suddenly dawned on me. Sometimes on holidays I would go to Nevsky Prospect between three and four, and stroll along the sunny side. That is, I by no means went strolling there, but experienced countless torments, humiliations, and risings of bile; that must have been just what I needed. I darted like an eel among the passers-by, in a most uncomely fashion, ceaselessly giving way now to generals, now to cavalry officers and hussars, now to ladies; in those moments I felt convulsive pains in my heart and a hotness in my spine at the mere thought of the measliness of my attire and the measliness and triteness of my darting little figure. This was a torment of torments, a ceaseless, unbearable humiliation from the thought, which would turn into a ceaseless and immediate sensation, of my being a fly before that whole world, a foul, obscene fly—more intelligent, more developed, more noble than everyone else—that went without saying—but a fly, ceaselessly giving way to everyone, humiliated by everyone, insulted by everyone. Why I gathered this torment onto myself, why I went to Nevsky—I don't know, I was simply *drawn* there at every opportunity.

I was then already beginning to experience the influxes of those pleasures of which I have already spoken in the first chapter. And after the story with the officer, I began to be drawn there even more strongly: it was on Nevsky that I met him most often, it was there that I admired him. He, too, used mostly to go there on holidays. And he, too, swerved out of the way before generals and persons of dignity, and he, too, slipped among them like an eel, but those of our sort, or even better than our sort, he simply crushed; he went straight at them as if there were an empty space before him, and on no occasion gave way to them. I reveled in my spite as I watched him, and . . . each time spitefully swerved out of his way. It tormented me that even in the street I simply could not be on an equal footing with him. "Why is it invariably you who swerve first?" I kept nagging at myself, in furious hysterics, sometimes waking up, say, between two and three in the morning. "Why precisely you and not him? There's no law that says so, it's not written anywhere? Well, then let it be equal, as is usual when men of delicacy meet: he can yield by half, and you by half, and so you will pass mutually respecting each other." But it was never so, and I still kept swerving, and he did not even notice that I was giving way to him. And then a most astonishing thought suddenly dawned on me. "What," I fancied, "what if I meet him and . . . do not step aside? Deliberately do not step aside, even if I have to shove him—eh? how will that be?" This bold thought gradually took such possession of me that it left me no peace. I dreamed of it ceaselessly, terribly, and deliberately went more often to Nevsky, to picture more clearly how I was going to do it when I did it. I was in ecstasy. The intention seemed more and more probable and possible to me. "Not really to shove him, of course," I thought, growing kinder in advance from joy, "but just so, simply not to give way, to bump into him, not so very painfully, but so, shoulder against shoulder, only as much as decency warrants, so that exactly as much as he bumps me, I will also bump him." I was, finally, completely decided on it. But the preparations took a very long time. First of all, at the time of the performance one had to look as decent as possible and see to one's attire. "Just in case, supposing, for example, that a public incident should get started (and the public there is *superflu*:[7] a countess goes, Prince D. goes, the whole of literature goes), one must be well dressed; this makes an impression, and in some sense will put us straightaway on an equal footing in the eyes of high society." To that end I asked for an advance on my salary and bought black gloves and a respectable hat at Churkin's. Black gloves, it seemed to me, were both more imposing and more in bon ton than the lemon-colored ones I had first presumed upon. "The color is too striking, it's too much as if a man wants to make a show of himself," and I did not buy the lemon ones. I had long since prepared a good shirt with white bone cuff-links; but I was very much detained by the overcoat. My overcoat was not bad at all in itself, it kept me warm; but it had a quilted cotton lining, and the collar was of raccoon, which constituted the height of lackeydom. It was necessary to change the collar at any cost and to acquire a beaver, something like what officers wore. For that I began walking about the Gostiny Arcade[8] and, after several attempts, set my sights on a cheap German beaver. Though these German beavers wear out very quickly and acquire a most measly look, at first, when new, they even seem quite decent; and I needed it for only one time. I asked the price: it was expensive even so. After some solid reflection I decided to sell my raccoon collar. And the remaining and for me quite considerable sum I decided to try and borrow from Anton Antonych Setochkin, my department chief, a humble but serious and positive man, who never loaned money to anyone, but to whom I had once, on entering my post, been especially recommended by the important personage who had placed me in the civil service. I was terribly tormented. To ask money of Anton Antonych seemed to me monstrous and shameful. I even could not sleep for two or three nights, but then I generally slept little at that time, I was in a fever; my heart was somehow vaguely sinking, or else it would suddenly start to go thump, thump, thump! . . . Anton Antonych was surprised at first, then he frowned, then he considered, and after all he gave me the loan, having me sign an authorization for him to take the loaned money from my salary two weeks later. Thus everything was finally ready; a handsome beaver came to reign in place of the squalid raccoon, and I gradually began to get down to business. I really couldn't just decide it straight off, slapdash; the thing had to be handled deftly, precisely gradually. But I confess that after many attempts I even began to despair: we simply couldn't bump into each other—and that was that! After all my preparations, after all my premeditations—it would look as if we were just about to bump into each other, and then—again I'd give way, and he would pass by without noticing me. I even recited prayers while approaching him, asking God to inspire me with decisiveness. One time I was already quite decided, but it just ended with me getting under his feet, because in the very last moment, at some two inches away, I lost courage. He quite calmly walked over me, and I bounced aside like a ball. That night I was sick again, feverish and delirious. And suddenly everything ended in the best possible way. The night before, I resolved finally not to carry out my pernicious intention and to let it all go for naught, and with that purpose in mind I went to Nevsky for the last time, just to see how I was going to let it all go for naught. Suddenly, within three steps of my enemy, I unexpectedly decided, closed my eyes, and—we bumped solidly shoulder against shoulder! I did not yield an inch and passed by on a perfectly equal footing! He did not even look back and pretended not to notice: but he only pretended, I'm sure of that. To this day I'm sure of it! Of course, I got the worst of it; he was stronger, but that was not the point. The point was that I had achieved my purpose, preserved my dignity, yielded not a step, and placed myself publicly on an equal social footing with him. I returned home perfectly avenged for everything. I was in ecstasy. I exulted and sang Italian arias. Of course, I shall not describe for you what happened to me three days later; if you've read my first chapter, "Underground," you can guess for yourself. The officer was later

transferred somewhere. I haven't seen him for about fourteen
years. What's the sweet fellow doing these days? Whom does
he crush now?

II

Then the spell of my little debauch would end, and
I'd feel terribly nauseated. Repentance would come; I'd
drive it away—it was too nauseating. Little by little, however,
I'd get used to that as well. I could get used to anything—that
is, not really get used, but somehow voluntarily consent to
endure it. But I had a way out that reconciled everything,
which was—to escape into "everything beautiful and lofty," in
dreams, of course. I dreamed terribly, I would dream for three
months at a time, shrinking into my corner, and, believe me,
in those moments I bore no resemblance to that gentleman
who, in the panic of his chicken heart, sat sewing a German
beaver to the collar of his overcoat. I'd suddenly become a
hero. And then I wouldn't even have let the six-foot lieutenant
into the house. I couldn't even imagine him then. What these
dreams of mine were, and how I could have been satisfied
with them—is difficult to say now, but I was satisfied with
them then. However, I'm somewhat satisfied with them even
now. Dreams came to me with a particular sweetness and
intensity after a little debauch, they came with repentance
and tears, with curses and raptures. There were moments of
such positive ecstasy, such happiness, that not even the slightest mockery could be felt in me, by God. There was faith,
hope, love. This was the point, that I blindly believed then
that through some miracle, some external circumstance, all
this would suddenly extend, expand; suddenly a horizon of
appropriate activity would present itself, beneficent, beautiful, and, above all, *quite ready-made* (precisely what, I never

knew, but above all—quite ready-made), and thus I would suddenly step forth under God's heaven all but on a white horse and wreathed in laurels. A secondary role was incomprehensible to me, and that was precisely why, in reality, I so calmly filled the last. Either hero or mud, there was no in-between. And that is what ruined me, because in the mud I comforted myself with being a hero at other times, and the hero covered up the mud: for an ordinary man, say, it's shameful to be muddied, but a hero is too lofty to be completely muddied, consequently one can get muddied. Remarkably, these influxes of "everything beautiful and lofty" used also to come to me during my little debauches; precisely when I was already at the very bottom, they would come just so, in isolated little flashes, as if reminding me of themselves, and yet they did not annihilate the little debauch with their appearance; on the contrary, it was as if they enlivened it by contrast and came in exactly the proportion required for a good sauce. The sauce here consisted of contradiction and suffering, of tormenting inner analysis, and all these torments and tormenticules lent my little debauch a certain piquancy, even meaning—in short, they fully fulfilled the function of a good sauce. All this was even not without some profundity. For how could I consent to a simple, direct, trite little scrivener's debauch, and to bearing all this mud on myself! What was there in it that could seduce me and lure me into the streets at night? No, sir, I had a noble loophole for everything . . .

But how much love, Lord, how much love I used to experience in those dreams of mine, in those "escapes into everything beautiful and lofty": though it was a fantastical love, though it was never in reality applied to anything human, there was so much of it, this love, that afterwards, in reality, I never even felt any need to apply it; that would have been an unnecessary luxury. Everything, however, would always end most happily with a lazy and rapturous transition to art—that is, to beautiful forms of being, quite ready-made, highly stolen from poets and novelists, and adapted to every possible service or demand. For example, I triumph over everyone; everyone, of course, is lying in the dust and is forced to voluntarily acknowledge all my perfections, and I forgive them all. I fall in love, being a famous poet and court chamberlain; I receive countless millions and donate them immediately to mankind, and then and there confess before all the world my disgraces, which, of course, are not mere disgraces, but contain an exceeding amount of "the beautiful and lofty," of something manfredian.[9] Everyone weeps and kisses me (what blockheads they'd be otherwise), and I go barefoot and hungry to preach new ideas and crush the retrograde under Austerlitz.[10] Then a march is struck up, an amnesty is granted, the Pope agrees to quit Rome for Brazil; then a ball is given for the whole of Italy at the Villa Borghese, now on the shores of Lake Como, since Lake Como has been transferred to Rome especially for the occasion;[11] then comes a scene in the bushes, etc., etc.—you know what I mean! You will say that it's vulgar and vile to bring all this out into the marketplace now, after so many raptures and tears, to which I myself have confessed. But why is it vile, sirs? Can you really think I'm ashamed of it all, or that it's all any stupider than whatever there may have been, gentlemen, in your own lives? And besides, believe me, some of it was by no means badly composed . . . And not all of it took place on Lake Como. However, you're right, it is indeed both vulgar and vile. And what's vilest is that I've now started justifying myself before you. And viler still is that I'm now making this remark. Enough, however; otherwise there will be no end to it: things will go on getting viler and viler . . .

I was simply incapable of dreaming for longer than three months at a time, and would begin to feel an irresistible need to rush into society. To rush into society in my case meant to go and visit my department chief, Anton Antonych Setoch-kin. He was the only permanent acquaintance I've had in my whole life, and I'm even surprised now at this circum-stance. But even to him I used to go only when such a spell came, and my dreams had reached such happiness that I needed, instantly and infallibly, to embrace people and the whole of mankind—for which I had to have available at least one really existing person. Anton Antonych, however, could be visited only on Tuesdays (his day), and consequently my need to embrace the whole of mankind always had to be ad-justed to a Tuesday. This Anton Antonych was located near the Five Corners,[12] on the fourth floor and in four little rooms, low-ceilinged, each one smaller than the last, of a most eco-nomical and yellow appearance. There were two daughters and their aunt, who poured tea. The daughters, one thirteen and the other fourteen, were both pug-nosed, and I was ter-ribly abashed before them, because they constantly whispered together and giggled. The host usually sat in the study, on a leather sofa in front of the desk, along with some gray-haired guest, an official from our own or even some other depart-ment. I never saw more than two or three guests there, always the same ones. They talked about excise, negotiations in the Senate, salaries, promotions, His Excellency, ways of making oneself liked, and so on and so forth. I had patience enough to sit it out by these people like a fool for four hours on end, listening to them, myself not daring or knowing how to begin talking with them about anything. My mind would grow dull, I'd break into a sweat several times, paralysis hovered over me; but this was good and beneficial. On returning home, I'd put off for a while my desire to embrace the whole of mankind.

I had, however, another acquaintance as it were—Simonov, a former schoolfellow. No doubt there were many of my schoolfellows in Petersburg, but I did not associate with them, and had even stopped nodding to them in the street. I perhaps got myself transferred to another department so as not to be together with them and to cut off all at once the whole of that hateful childhood of mine. Curses on that school, on those terrible years of penal servitude! In short, I parted ways with my fellows as soon as I was set free. There were two or three people left whom I still greeted when we met. Among them was Simonov, who had not been distinguished for anything in our school, was quiet and equable, but in whom I distinguished a certain independence of character and even honesty. I do not even think he was so very narrow-minded. I had once had some rather bright moments with him, but they did not last long and somehow suddenly clouded over. These recollections were apparently burdensome for him, and it seemed he kept being afraid I would lapse into the former tone. I suspected that he found me quite disgusting, but I kept going to him all the same, having no sure assurance of it.

And so once, on a Thursday, unable to endure my solitude, and knowing that on Thursdays Anton Antonych's door was closed, I remembered about Simonov. On the way up to his fourth-floor apartment, I was precisely thinking that I was a burden to this gentleman and that I shouldn't be going to him. But since in the end such considerations, as if by design, always egged me on further into some ambiguous situation, I did go in. It was almost a year since I had last seen Simonov.

III

I FOUND TWO MORE of my schoolfellows with him. They were apparently discussing an important matter. None of them paid more than the slightest attention to my coming, which was even strange, because I hadn't seen them for years. Obviously they regarded me as something like a quite ordinary fly. I had not been treated that way even at school, though everyone there hated me. Of course, I understood that they must scorn me now for the unsuccess of my career in the service and for my having gone too much to seed, walking around badly dressed, and so on—which in their eyes constituted a signboard of my incapacity and slight significance. But all the same I did not expect such a degree of scorn. Simonov was even surprised at my coming. Before, too, he had always seemed surprised at my coming. All this took me aback; I sat down in some anguish and began to listen to what they were talking about.

The conversation, a serious and even heated one, was about a farewell dinner which these gentlemen wanted to organize jointly on the very next day for their schoolfellow Zverkov, an officer in the army, who was leaving for a province far away. M'sieur Zverkov had also been my schoolfellow all the while. I had begun especially to hate him starting in the higher grades. In the lower grades he had been just a pretty, frisky boy whom everybody liked. I, however, had hated him in the lower grades as well, precisely for being a pretty and frisky boy. He was always a bad student, and got worse as he went on. Nevertheless, he graduated successfully, because he had his protectors. In his last year at school he received an inheritance, two hundred souls,[13] and since we were almost all of us poor, he even began to swagger before us. He was a vulgarian in the highest degree, but a nice fellow nonetheless, even while swaggering. And despite the external, fantastic, and highfalutin forms of honor and glory in our school, everyone, apart from a very few, minced around Zverkov, the more so the more he swaggered. They minced not for the sake of some sort of profit, but just so, because he was a man favored with the gifts of nature. Besides, it was somehow an accepted thing among us to regard Zverkov as an expert in the line of adroitness and good manners. This last particularly infuriated me. I hated the sharp, un-self-doubting tone of his voice, his admiration of his own witticisms, which came out terribly stupid, though he did have a bold tongue; I hated his handsome but silly face (for which, by the way, I'd gladly have traded my *intelligent* one) and his free and easy officer-of-the-forties airs. I hated the things he used to say about his future successes with women (he hadn't ventured to start up with women, not having his officer's epaulettes yet, and was looking forward to them impatiently) and about how he'd be fighting duels all the time. I remember myself, always taciturn, suddenly lighting into Zverkov when he was talking with some friends about his future gallantries once during a recess, got quite playful in the end, like a puppy in the sun, and suddenly declared that he wouldn't leave a single village maiden on his estate without his attentions, that this was his *droit de seigneur*,[14] and if the peasants dared to protest, he'd give them all a whipping and heap a double quitrent on the bearded canaille. Our oafs applauded, but I lit into him, and not at all out of pity for maidens or their fathers, but simply because such a little snot was being so applauded. I got the best of him that time, but Zverkov, though stupid, was gay and impudent, and therefore laughed it off, and even in such a way that, in truth, I did not quite get the best of him: the laughter remained on his side. Later he got the best of me several more times, though not with spite, but just somehow jokingly, in passing, with a laugh. I spitefully and contemptuously refused to reply. Upon graduation he tried to make a step towards me; I did not resist too much, because it flattered me; but we quickly and naturally parted ways. Later I heard about his barracksy-lieutenanty successes, about his *carousing*. Later other rumors went around—that he was *succeeding* in the service. Now he no longer greeted me in the street, and I suspected he was afraid of compromising himself by greeting a person as insignificant as I was. I also saw him in the theater once, in the third circle, now wearing aiguillettes. He was mincing and twining around the daughters of some ancient general. In three short years he had gone very much to seed, though he was still quite handsome and adroit; he had become somehow puffy and was beginning to grow fat; one could see that by the age of thirty he would be completely flabby. It was for this finally departing Zverkov that our fellows wanted to give a dinner. They had constantly associated with him all those three years, though inwardly they did not consider themselves on an equal footing with him, I'm sure of that.

Of Simonov's two guests, one was Ferfichkin, from Russian-German stock—short, monkey-faced, a fool who comically mimicked everyone, my bitterest enemy even in the lower grades—a mean, impudent little fanfaron who played at being most ticklishly ambitious, though of course he was a coward at heart. He was one of those admirers of Zverkov who flirted with him for his own ends, and often borrowed money from him. Simonov's other guest, Trudolyubov, was an unremarkable person, a military type, tall, with a cold physiognomy, honest enough, but worshiping any success, and capable only of discussing promotions. He was some sort of distant relation of Zverkov's, and that, silly though it was, endowed him with a certain significance among us. He had always regarded me as nothing, but treated me, if not quite politely, at least passably.

"Well, so, if it's seven roubles each," Trudolyubov said, "that makes twenty-one for the three of us—we can have a nice dinner. Zverkov doesn't pay, of course."

"Naturally not, since we're inviting him," Simonov decided.

"Do you really think," Ferfichkin broke in presumptuously and fervently, like an impudent lackey boasting of his master's, the general's, decorations, "do you really think Zverkov will let us pay for it all? He'll accept out of delicacy, but he'll stand us to a *half-dozen* himself."

"And what are the four of us going to do with a half-dozen," Trudolyubov remarked, having paid attention only to the half-dozen.

"So, it's the three of us, four with Zverkov, twenty-one roubles, the Hôtel de Paris, tomorrow at five o'clock," Simonov, who had been elected manager, finally concluded.

"Why twenty-one?" I said, somewhat agitated, apparently even offended. "If you count me, it's twenty-eight roubles, not twenty-one."

It seemed to me that to offer myself suddenly and so unexpectedly would even be a most handsome thing, and they would all be won over at once and look upon me with respect.

"You want to come, too?" Simonov remarked with displeasure, somehow avoiding my eyes. He knew me by heart.

It infuriated me that he knew me by heart.

"What of it, sir? I would seem to be a schoolfellow, too, and I confess I'm even offended at being left out," I began seething again.

"And where does one go looking for you?" Ferfichkin rudely butted in.

"You were never on good terms with Zverkov," Trudolyubov added, frowning. But once I had fastened on, I would not let go.

"It seems to me that no one has any right to judge about that," I retorted, in a trembling voice, as if God knows what had happened. "Maybe that's precisely why I want to now, because we weren't on good terms before."

"Well, who can understand you . . . and these sublimities . . ." Trudolyubov smirked.

"You'll be put on the list," Simonov decided, turning to me. "Tomorrow, five o'clock, the Hôtel de Paris; make no mistake."

"And the money!" Ferfichkin tried to begin, in a half-whisper, nodding towards me to Simonov, but he stopped short, because even Simonov became embarrassed.

"Enough," said Trudolyubov, rising. "Let him come, if he wants to so much."

"But we have our own circle, we're friends," Ferfichkin, angry, was also reaching for his hat. "This isn't an official meeting. Maybe we don't want you at all . . ."

They left; Ferfichkin did not even bow to me as he went out; Trudolyubov barely nodded, without looking. Simonov, with whom I was left face to face, was in some sort of annoyed perplexity and gave me a strange glance. He did not sit down, nor did he invite me to sit down.

"Hm . . . yes . . . tomorrow, then. And will you give me the money now? Just to know for certain," he muttered in embarrassment.

I flushed, but as I flushed I recalled that I had owed Simonov fifteen roubles from time immemorial, which, however, I had never forgotten, though I also had never repaid it.

"You must see, Simonov, that I couldn't have known on coming here . . . and I'm very annoyed with myself for forgetting . . ."

"All right, all right, never mind. You can pay tomorrow at dinner. I just wanted to know . . . Please don't . . ."

He stopped short and began pacing the room with even greater annoyance. As he paced, he started planting his heels and stomping still more heavily.

"I'm not keeping you, am I?" I asked, after a two-minute silence.

"Oh, no!" he suddenly roused himself, "that is, to tell the truth—yes. You see, I've also got to stop by at . . . Not far from here . . ." he added, in a sort of apologetic voice, and somewhat ashamedly.

"Ah, my God! Why didn't you say so!" I exclaimed, grabbing my cap, but with an appearance of remarkable non-chalance, which flew down to me from God knows where.

"It's not far, really . . . Just a couple of steps . . ." Simonov kept saying as he saw me to the entryway with a bustling air that did not become him at all. "Tomorrow, then, at five o'clock sharp!" he called out as I went down the stairs: he was so pleased I was leaving. I, however, was furious.

"What possessed me, what possessed me to pop up like that!" I gnashed my teeth, striding along the street. "And for that scoundrel, that little pig of a Zverkov! I mustn't go, of course; just spit on it, of course; I'm not bound, am I? Tomorrow I'll send Simonov a note . . ."

But what made me furious was that I knew I would certainly go; I would go on purpose; and the more tactless, the more improper it was for me to go, the sooner I would go.

And there was even a positive obstacle to my going: I had no money. All I had lying there was nine roubles. But of that, seven had to go the next day for the wages of Apollon, my servant, who lived with me for seven roubles a month, grub not included.

And not to pay him his wages was impossible, given Apollon's character. But of this dog, this thorn in my side, I will speak some other time.

Nevertheless, I knew that even so I would not pay him, but would certainly go.

That night I had the most hideous dreams. No wonder: all evening I was oppressed by recollections of the penal servitude of my school years, and I could not get rid of them. I had been tucked away in that school by distant relations whose dependent I was and of whom I had no notion thereafter—tucked away, orphaned, already beaten down by their reproaches, already pensive, taciturn, gazing wildly about at everything. My schoolfellows met me with spiteful and merciless derision, because I was not like any of them. But I could not endure derision; I could not get along so cheaply as they got along with each other. I immediately began to hate them, and shut myself away from everyone in timorous, wounded, and inordinate pride. Their crudeness outraged me. They laughed cynically at my face, my ungainly figure; and yet how stupid their own faces were! In our school facial expressions degenerated and would become somehow especially stupid. So many beautiful children came to us. A few years later it was disgusting even to look at them. Already at the age of sixteen I gloomily marveled at them; even then I was amazed at the pettiness of their thinking, the stupidity of their pastimes, games, conversations. They had so little understanding of the most essential things, so little interest in the most impressive, startling subjects, that I began, willy-nilly, to regard them as beneath me. It was not injured vanity that prompted me to do so, and for God's sake don't come creeping at me with those banal objections that one is sick of to the point of nausea—"that I was only dreaming, while they already understood real life." They understood nothing, no real life, and I swear it was this in them that outraged me most of all. On the contrary, they took the most obvious, glaring reality in a fantastically stupid way, and were already accustomed to worshiping success alone. Everything that was just, but humiliated and downtrodden, they laughed at disgracefully and hardheartedly. They regarded rank as intelligence; at the age of sixteen they were already talking about cushy billets. Of course, much of this came from stupidity, from the bad examples that had ceaselessly surrounded their childhood and adolescence. They were depraved to the point of monstrosity. To be sure, here, too, there was more of the external, more of an assumed cynicism; to be sure, youthfulness and a certain freshness could be glimpsed in them even through the depravity; but even this freshness was unattractive in them and showed itself as a sort of knavery. I hated them terribly, though I was perhaps worse than they were. They paid me back in kind and did not conceal their loathing for me. But I no longer had any wish for their love; on the contrary, I constantly thirsted for their humiliation. To rid myself of their derision, I purposely began to study as hard as I could and worked my way into the number of the best. This made an impression. Besides, they began little by little to realize that I had by then read such books as they were unable to read, and understood such things (not part of our special course) as they had never even heard of. This they regarded wildly and derisively, but morally they submitted, the more so as even the teachers paid attention to me in this respect. The derision stopped, but the animosity remained, and cold, strained relations set in. Towards the end I myself could not stand it: as I grew older, a need for people, for friends, developed. I tried to start getting closer with some; but the attempt always came out unnaturally and would simply end of itself. I also once had a friend. But I was already a despot in my soul; I wanted to have unlimited power over his soul; I wanted to instill in him a contempt for his surrounding milieu; I demanded of him a haughty and final break with that milieu. I frightened him with my passionate friendship; I drove him to tears, to convulsions; he was a naive, self-giving soul; but once he had given himself wholly to me, I immediately started to hate him and pushed him away—as if I had needed him only to gain a victory over him, only to bring him into subjection. But I could not be victorious over everyone; my friend was also not like any of them, and represented the rarest exception. The first thing I did upon leaving school was quit the special service for which I had been intended, in order to break all ties, to curse the past and bury it in the dust . . . And the devil knows why, after that, I dragged myself to this Simonov! . . .

In the morning I roused myself early, I jumped out of bed in agitation, as if all this was going to start happening right away. But then I did believe that some radical break in my life was coming and could not fail to come that very day. It may have been lack of habit or something, but all my life, when faced with any external event, be it ever so small, I always thought that right then some radical break in my life was going to come. Nevertheless, I went to work as usual, but slipped away two hours early to go home and get ready. The main thing, I thought, is that I mustn't be the first to arrive, or they'll think I'm all too delighted. But there were thousands of such main things, and they all agitated me to the point of impotence. I polished my boots a second time with my own hands; for the life of him Apollon would not have polished them twice in one day, finding it inordinate. I polished them, therefore, having stolen the brushes from the entryway so that he would not somehow notice and afterwards begin to despise me. Then I carefully inspected my clothes and found that everything was old, shabby, worn out. I had indeed become too slovenly. My uniform was perhaps in good condition, but I really couldn't go to dinner in my uniform. And the main thing was that on my trousers, right on the knee, there was a huge yellow spot. I could sense already that this spot alone would rob me of nine-tenths of my dignity. I also knew that it was very mean to think so. "But I can't be bothered with thinking now; now comes reality," I thought, and my heart sank. I also knew perfectly well, even then, that I was monstrously exaggerating all these facts; but there was nothing to be done: I could no longer control myself, I was shaking with fever. In despair I pictured how coldly and condescendingly that "scoundrel" Zverkov would meet me; with what dull, all-invincible contempt the dullard Trudolyubov would look at me; how nastily and impudently that little snot Ferfichkin would titter at my expense, sucking up to Zverkov; how perfectly Simonov would understand it all in himself, and how he would despise me for the meanness of my vanity and faintheartedness; and, the main thing—how measly, non-*literary*, commonplace it was all going to be. Of course, it would be best not to go at all. But that was more impossible than anything else: once I began to be drawn, I used to be drawn in all the way, over my head. Afterwards I'd have been taunting myself for the rest of my life: "So you turned coward, turned coward before *reality*, that's what you did, you turned coward!" On the contrary, I passionately wanted to prove to all that "riffraff" that I was by no means the coward I made myself out to be. More than that: in the strongest paroxysm of cowardly fever, I dreamed of getting the best of them, winning them over, carrying them away, making them love me—if only for my "lofty mind and indubitable wit." They would drop Zverkov, he would sit on the sidelines, silent and ashamed, and I would crush him. Afterwards I would perhaps make peace with him, and we would pledge eternal friendship, yet the most bitter and offensive thing for me was that I knew even then, knew fully and certainly, that in fact I needed none of that, and in fact I had no wish to crush, subject, or attract them, and would be the first not to give a penny for the whole outcome, even if I achieved it. Oh, how I prayed to God for that day to pass more quickly! In inexpressible anguish I kept going to the window, opening the vent, and peering into the dull darkness of thickly falling wet snow . . .

At last my wretched little wall clock hissed five. I grabbed my hat and, trying not to glance at Apollon—who since morning had been waiting to receive his wages from me, but in his pride refused to speak first—slipped past him out the door, and in a coach hired for the purpose with my last fifty kopecks, drove up like a grand gentleman to the Hôtel de Paris.

IV

I HAD ALREADY KNOWN the evening before that I would be the first to arrive. But primacy was no longer the point. Not only were none of them there, but I even had difficulty finding our room. The table was not quite laid yet. What did it mean? After much questioning, I finally got out of the waiters that the dinner had been ordered for six o'clock, not five. This was confirmed in the bar. I was even ashamed to be asking. It was only five twenty-five. If they had changed the time, they ought in any case to have informed me; that's what the city mail is for; and not to have subjected me to "disgrace" both in my own and . . . be it only the waiters' eyes. I sat down; a waiter began laying the table; in his presence it felt somehow still more offensive. By six o'clock, in addition to the lighted lamps, candles were brought into the room. It had not occurred to the waiter, however, to bring them when I arrived. In the next room two customers, gloomy, angry-looking, and silent, were having dinner at separate tables. In one of the farther rooms it was very noisy; there was even shouting; the guffaws of a whole bunch of people could be heard; some nasty French squeals could be heard: it was a dinner with ladies. Quite nauseating, in short. Rarely have I spent a nastier moment, so that when, at exactly six o'clock, they all came in together, I was glad of them for the first moment as of some sort of deliverers, and almost forgot that I ought to look offended.

Zverkov came at the head of them, obviously the leader. Both he and they were laughing; but on seeing me Zverkov assumed a dignified air, approached unhurriedly, bending slightly, as if coquettishly, at the waist, and gave me his hand benignly, but not very, with a certain cautious, almost senatorial politeness, as if by offering me his hand he were protecting himself from something. I had been imagining, on the contrary, that as soon as he walked in he would start laughing his former laugh, shrill, punctuated by little shrieks, and from the first there would be his flat jokes and witticisms. I had been preparing myself for them since the previous evening, but I by no means expected such down-the-nose, such excellential benignity. So he now fully considered himself immeasurably superior to me in all respects? If he simply wanted to offend me with this senatorial air, it was not so bad, I thought; I'd be able to get back at him somehow. But what if indeed, without any wish to offend me, the little idea had seriously crept into his sheep's noddle that he was immeasurably superior to me, and could look at me in no other way than patronizingly? The supposition alone left me breathless.

"I learned with surprise of your wish to participate with us," he began, lisping and simpering and drawing the words out, something that had never happened with him before. "We somehow keep missing each other. You shy away from us. More's the pity. We're not so terrible as you think. Well, sir, in any case I'm gla-a-ad to rene-e-ew . . ."

And he casually turned to place his hat on the windowsill.

"Have you been waiting long?" asked Trudolyubov.

"I arrived at exactly five o'clock, as I was appointed yesterday," I answered loudly and with an irritation that promised an imminent explosion.

"Didn't you inform him that the time had been changed?" Trudolyubov turned to Simonov.

"I didn't. I forgot," the latter answered, but without any repentance, and, not even apologizing to me, went to make arrangements for the hors d'oeuvres.

"So you've been here for an hour already, ah, poor fellow!" Zverkov exclaimed derisively, because according to his notions it must indeed have been terribly funny. Following him, the scoundrel Ferfichkin broke up, in his scoundrelly voice, yelping like a little mutt. He, too, thought my situation terribly funny and embarrassing.

"It's not funny in the least!" I cried to Ferfichkin, growing more and more irritated. "It's other people's fault, not mine. They neglected to inform me. It—it—it's . . . simply absurd."

"Not only absurd, but something else as well," Trudolyubov grumbled, naively interceding for me. "You're too mild. Sheer discourtesy. Not deliberate, of course. But how is it that Simonov . . . hm!"

"If that had been played on me," observed Ferfichkin, "I'd . . ."

"But you should have ordered yourself something," Zverkov interrupted, "or just asked to have dinner without waiting."

"You must agree that I could have done so without any permission," I snapped. "If I waited, it was . . ."

"Let's be seated, gentlemen," cried the entering Simonov, "everything's ready; I can answer for the champagne, it's perfectly chilled . . . I didn't know your address, how was one to find you?" he suddenly turned to me, but again somehow without looking at me. He obviously had something against me. He must have changed his mind since yesterday.

Everyone sat down; I, too, sat down. The table was round. Trudolyubov ended up on my left, Simonov on my right. Zverkov sat down across the table, and Ferfichkin next to him, between him and Trudolyubov.

"So-o-o, you're . . . in the department?" Zverkov continued to occupy himself with me. Seeing that I was embarrassed, he seriously imagined I must be treated benignly and, so to speak, encouraged. "What, does he want me to throw a bottle at him or something?" I thought, furious. From lack of habit, I was becoming irritated with a somehow unnatural rapidity.

"In the ——y office," I answered curtly, staring at my plate.

"And . . . you fffind it profffitable? Tell me, ple-e-ease, what wa-a-as it that made you leave your former position?"

"It wa-a-a-as that I felt like leaving my former position," I drawled three times longer, now losing almost all control of myself. Ferfichkin snorted. Simonov looked at me ironically; Trudolyubov stopped eating and began studying me with curiosity.

Zverkov winced, but declined to notice.

"We-e-ell, and how's your keep?"

"What keep?"

"Your sssalary, that is."

"Quite the examiner, aren't you!"

However, I told him straight out what my salary was. I was blushing terribly.

"Not a fortune," Zverkov observed pompously.

"No, sir, can't go dining in café-restaurants!" Ferfichkin added impudently.

"In my opinion, it's even downright poor," Trudolyubov observed seriously.

"And how thin you've grown, how changed . . . since . . ." Zverkov added, not without venom now, studying me and my attire with a sort of insolent regret.

"Oh, come, stop embarrassing him," Ferfichkin exclaimed, tittering.

"My dear sir, I'll have you know that I am not embarrassed," I finally exploded, "do you hear, sir! I am having dinner here, in a 'café-restaurant,' at my own expense, my own and no one else's, make a note of that, Monsieur Ferfichkin."

"Wha-a-at? And who here is not dining at his own expense? If you mean to . . ." Ferfichkin fastened on, turning red as a lobster and staring me furiously in the face.

"We-e-ell," I replied, feeling that I had gone too far, "I

suppose we'd better occupy ourselves with more intelligent conversation."

"So you intend to display your intelligence?"

"Don't worry, that would be quite superfluous here."

"You just keep cackling away, eh, my dear sir? Haven't lost your mind, by any chance, in that de*pot*ment of yours?"

"Enough, gentlemen, enough!" Zverkov cried almightily.

"How stupid this is!" growled Simonov.

"Stupid indeed; we gathered as a company of friends to see a good school chum off on his journey, and you go keeping score," Trudolyubov began to speak, rudely addressing me alone. "You invited yourself yesterday, so don't disrupt the general harmony . . ."

"Enough, enough," Zverkov shouted. "Stop, gentlemen, this won't do. Better let me tell you how I almost got married two days ago . . ."

And there followed some lampoon about how the gentleman almost got married two days before. There was, however, not a word in it about marriage, but generals, colonels, and even court dignitaries kept flitting through the story, with Zverkov among them and all but at their head. Approving laughter began; Ferfichkin even let out little squeals.

They all dropped me, and I sat crushed and annihilated.

"Lord, is this any company for me!" I thought. "And what a fool I made of myself before them! However, I let Ferfichkin go too far. These oafs think they've done me an honor by giving me a place at their table; they don't realize that it's I, I, who am doing them an honor, and not they me! 'How thin! Such clothes!' Oh, cursed trousers! Zverkov has already noticed the yellow spot on the knee . . . But what's the point! Get up from the table, now, this minute, take your hat, and simply leave without saying a word . . . Out of scorn! And tomorrow, if they like, a duel. Scoundrels. Am I going to be sorry about seven roubles? Maybe they'll think . . . Devil take it! I'm not sorry about the seven roubles! I'm leaving this minute! . . ."

Of course, I stayed.

I drank Lafite and sherry by the glassful in my grief. From lack of habit I was quickly getting drunk, and as my drunkenness increased, so did my vexation. I suddenly wanted to insult them all in the boldest fashion, and only then leave. To seize the right moment and show myself; let them say: he's funny, but no dummy . . . and . . . and . . . in short, devil take them!

I insolently looked around at them all with bleary eyes. But it was as if they had already forgotten me entirely . . . They were having a noisy, loud, merry time *for themselves*. Zverkov kept on talking. I began to listen. Zverkov was telling about some magnificent lady whom he had finally driven to a declaration (naturally he was lying like a horse), and that he had been especially helped in this matter by his intimate friend, some princeling named Kolya, a hussar, owner of three thousand souls.

"And yet there's no sign of this Kolya, owner of three thousand souls, at your farewell party," I suddenly butted in to the conversation. For a moment everyone fell silent.

"So, now you're drunk," Trudolyubov finally consented to notice me, casting a sidelong, contemptuous glance in my direction. Zverkov silently studied me as if I were a little bug. I lowered my eyes. Simonov hurriedly began pouring champagne.

Trudolyubov raised his glass; everyone did the same, except for me.

"Your health, and a good journey!" he cried to Zverkov. "To those old years, gentlemen, to our future! Hurrah!"

Everyone drank and fell to kissing Zverkov. I did not budge; the full glass stood untouched before me.

"You're not going to drink?" Trudolyubov, having lost all patience, roared, turning to me threateningly.

"I wish to make a speech on my own part, separately . . . and then I will drink, Mr. Trudolyubov."

"Disgusting little stinker," Simonov growled.

I straightened up on my chair and feverishly took my glass, preparing for something extraordinary, and still not knowing myself precisely what I was going to say.

"*Silence!*" Ferfichkin called out in French. "Here comes all kinds of intelligence!" Zverkov listened very seriously, realizing what was going on.

"Lieutenant Zverkov, sir," I began, "let it be known to you that I hate phrases, phrase-mongers, and tight-fitting waists . . . That is the first point, and the second will follow forthwith."

Everyone stirred greatly.

"Second point: I hate gallantry and gallantizers. Especially gallantizers!

"Third point: I love truth, sincerity, and honesty," I went on almost mechanically, because I was already beginning to go numb with horror, unable to understand how I could be speaking this way . . . "I love thought, M'sieur Zverkov; I love true friendship, on an equal footing, and not . . . hm . . . I love . . . However, why not? I, too, shall drink to your health, M'sieur Zverkov. Charm the Circassian girls, shoot the enemies of the fatherland, and . . . and . . . To your health, M'sieur Zverkov!"

Zverkov rose from his chair, bowed to me, and said:

"Much obliged to you."

He was terribly offended, and even turned pale.

"Devil take it," roared Trudolyubov, banging his fist on the table.

"No, sir, it's a punch in the mug for that!" Ferfichkin shrieked.

"He ought to be thrown out!" Simonov growled.

"Not a word, gentlemen, not a move!" Zverkov cried solemnly, checking the general indignation. "I thank you all, but I myself am quite capable of proving to him how much I value his words."

"Mr. Ferfichkin, tomorrow you will give me satisfaction for your present words!" I said loudly, pompously addressing Ferfichkin.

"You mean a duel, sir? At your pleasure," the man answered, but I must have been so ridiculous with my challenge, and it was so unsuited to my figure, that everyone, and finally even Ferfichkin, simply fell over laughing.

"Yes, drop him, of course! He's completely drunk now!" Trudolyubov said with loathing.

"I'll never forgive myself for putting him on the list!" Simonov growled again.

"Now's the time to up and hurl a bottle at them all," I thought, took the bottle, and . . . poured myself a full glass.

". . . No, I'd better sit it out to the end!" I went on thinking. "You'd be glad, gentlemen, if I left. No chance of that. I'll purposely sit and drink to the end, as a sign that I attach not the slightest importance to you. I'll sit and drink, because this is a pot-house, and I paid good money to get in. I'll sit and drink, because I regard you as pawns, nonexistent pawns. I'll sit and drink . . . and sing, if I like, yes, sirs, and sing, because I have the right . . . to sing . . . hm."

But I did not sing. I simply tried not to look at any of them; I assumed the most independent attitudes and waited impatiently for them to start talking to me *first*. But, alas, they didn't. And, oh, how I wished, how I wished at that moment to make peace with them! It struck eight o'clock, and finally nine. They moved from the table to the sofa. Zverkov sprawled on the couch, placing one foot on a little round table. The wine was also transferred there. Indeed, he did stand them to three bottles of his own. He did not offer me

any, of course. Everyone sat clustered around him on the sofa.
They listened to him with all but reverence. One could see he
was loved. "But why? Why?" I kept thinking to myself. From
time to time they would get into drunken raptures and kiss
each other. They talked about the Caucasus, about what true
passion is, about gambling, about profitable posts in the service; about how big was the income of the hussar Podkhar-
zhevsky, whom none of them knew personally, and rejoiced
that it was very big; about the remarkable beauty and grace
of Princess D——, whom none of them had ever even seen;
finally it came to Shakespeare being immortal.

I was smiling contemptuously and pacing the other side of
the room, directly opposite the sofa, along the wall, from the
table to the stove and back. I wished with all my might to
show that I could do without them; and yet I purposely
clumped with my boots, coming down hard on the heels. But
all in vain. *They* paid no attention. I had patience enough to
pace like that, right in front of them, from eight o'clock to
eleven, in one and the same space, from the table to the stove,
and from the stove back to the table. "I'm just pacing, and no
one can tell me not to." A waiter who kept coming into the
room paused several times to look at me; my head was spinning from so much turning; at moments I thought I was delirious. I sweated and dried out three times in those three
hours. Every once in a while a thought pierced my heart with
the deepest, most poisonous pain: that ten years, twenty years,
forty years would pass, and even after forty years I would still
recall with revulsion and humiliation these dirtiest, most ridiculous, and most terrible minutes of my entire life. For a
man to humiliate himself more shamelessly and more voluntarily was really impossible, I fully, fully understood that,
and still I went on pacing from the table to the stove and
back. "Oh, if you only knew what feelings and thoughts I'm
capable of, and how developed I am!" I thought at moments,

mentally addressing the sofa where my enemies were sitting.
But my enemies behaved as if I were not even in the room.
Once, once only, they turned to me—namely, when Zverkov
began talking about Shakespeare, and I suddenly guffawed
contemptuously. I snorted so affectedly and nastily that they
all broke off the conversation at once and silently watched
me for about two minutes, seriously, without laughing, as I
paced along the wall from table to stove and *paid no attention
to them.* But nothing came of it; they did not start talking to
me, and after two minutes dropped me again. It struck eleven.

"Gentlemen," cried Zverkov, rising from the sofa, "now
let us all go *there.*"

"Right, right!" the others began to say.

I turned sharply to Zverkov. I was so worn out, so broken,
that I had to finish it even if it killed me! I was in a fever; my
hair, wet with sweat, stuck to my forehead and temples.

"Zverkov! I ask your forgiveness," I said, abruptly and
resolutely, "yours too, Ferfichkin, and everyone's, everyone's, I've offended everyone!"

"Aha! So dueling's not your sport!" Ferfichkin hissed
venomously.

A sharp pain went through my heart.

"No, I'm not afraid of a duel, Ferfichkin! I'm ready to fight
you tomorrow, even after a reconciliation. I even insist on it,
and you cannot refuse me. I want to prove to you that I'm
not afraid of a duel. You'll have the first shot, and I'll shoot
into the air."

"He's indulging himself," remarked Simonov.

"Downright crackbrained!" echoed Trudolyubov.

"Let us pass, why're you standing in the way! . . . What
do you want?" Zverkov responded contemptuously. Their
faces were red; their eyes were shiny: they had drunk a lot.

"I ask your friendship, Zverkov, I offended you, but . . ."

"Y-y-you? Offended m-m-me? I'll have you know, my dear sir, that you could never under any circumstances offend *me*!"

"That's enough out of you. Step aside!" Trudolyubov clinched. "Let's go."

"Olympia's mine, gentlemen, it's agreed!" cried Zverkov.

"No objections! No objections!" they answered, laughing.

I stood there spat upon. The bunch noisily left the room. Trudolyubov struck up some stupid song. Simonov stayed behind for a tiny moment to tip the waiters. I suddenly went over to him.

"Simonov! Give me six roubles!" I said, resolutely and desperately.

He looked at me in extreme astonishment, his eyes somehow dull. He, too, was drunk.

"You want to go *there* with us, too?"

"Yes!"

"I have no money!" he snapped, grinned scornfully, and started out of the room.

I seized him by his overcoat. It was a nightmare.

"Simonov! I saw you had money, why do you refuse me? Am I a scoundrel? Beware of refusing me: if you knew, if you knew why I'm asking! Everything depends on it, my whole future, all my plans . . ."

Simonov took out the money and almost flung it at me.

"Take it, if you're so shameless!" he said pitilessly, and ran to catch up with them.

I remained alone for a moment. Disorder, leftovers, a broken wine glass on the floor, spilt wine, cigarette butts, drunkenness and delirium in my head, tormenting anguish in my heart, and, finally, the servant, who had seen everything and heard everything, and kept peeking curiously into my eyes.

"*There*!" I cried out. "Either they'll all fall on their knees, embrace my legs, and beg for my friendship, or . . . or I'll slap Zverkov's face!"

V

"HERE IT IS, here it is at last, the encounter with reality," I muttered, rushing headlong down the stairs. "This is no longer the Pope leaving Rome and going to Brazil; this is no longer a ball on Lake Como!"

"What a scoundrel you are," raced through my head, "to laugh at that now!"

"What of it!" I cried, answering myself. "All is lost now!"

Their trail was already cold; but no matter: I knew where they had gone.

By the porch stood a lonely jack, a night coachman, in a homespun coat all dusted with the still-falling wet and as if warm snow. It was steamy and stuffy. His shaggy little piebald nag was also all dusted with snow, and was coughing—I very much remember that. I rushed to the bast-covered sled; but as I raised my foot to get in, the recollection of the way Simonov had just given me the six roubles cut me down, and I dropped into the sled like a sack.

"No! Much must be done to redeem it all!" I cried out, "but I will redeem it, or perish on the spot this very night! Drive!"

We set off. A whole whirlwind was spinning in my head.

"Beg for my friendship on their knees—that they won't do. It's a mirage, a vulgar mirage, revolting, romantic, and fantastic; another ball on Lake Como. And therefore I *must* slap Zverkov's face! It's my duty. And so, it's decided; I'm flying now to slap his face."

"Faster!"

The jack started snapping the reins.

"I'll do it as soon as I walk in. Ought I to say a few words first, as a preface to the slap? No! I'll just walk in and slap him. They'll all be sitting in the drawing room, and he'll be on the sofa with Olympia. Cursed Olympia! She laughed at my face once and refused me. I'll pull Olympia by the hair, and Zverkov by the ears! No, better by one ear, and by that ear I'll lead him around the whole room. They'll probably all start beating me and kick me out. It's even certain. Let them! Still, I slapped him first: it was my initiative; and by the code of honor—that's everything; he's branded now, and no beating can wash away that slap, but only a duel. He'll have to fight. Yes, and let them beat me now. Let them, ignoble as they are! Trudolyubov especially will do the beating—he's so strong; Ferfichkin will fasten on from the side, and certainly grab my hair, that's sure. But let them, let them! I'm ready for it. Their sheep's noddles will finally be forced to grasp the tragic in it all! As they're dragging me to the door I'll cry out to them that in fact they're not worth my little finger."

"Faster, coachman, faster!" I shouted to the jack. He even jumped and swung his whip. For I shouted quite wildly.

"We'll fight at dawn, that's settled. It's all over with the department. Ferfichkin said de*pot*ment earlier instead of department. But where to get the pistols? Nonsense! I'll take an advance on my salary and buy them. And the powder, and the bullets? That's the second's affair. But how will I manage it all before dawn? And where will I find a second? I have no acquaintances . . . Nonsense!" I cried, whirling myself up even more, "nonsense! The first passer-by I speak to in the street is duty-bound to be my second, just like pulling a drowning man from the water. The most eccentric situations must be allowed for. Were I to ask even the director himself to be my second tomorrow, he, too, would have to agree out of knightly feelings alone, and keep the secret! Anton Antonych . . ."

The thing was that at the same moment I could see, more clearly and vividly than anyone else in the entire world, the whole, most odious absurdity of my suppositions, and the whole other side of the coin, but . . .

"Faster, coachman, faster, you rogue!"

"Eh, master!" said the backbone of the nation.

I suddenly felt cold all over.

"And wouldn't it be better . . . better . . . to go straight home now? Oh, my God! Why, why did I invite myself to this dinner yesterday! But no, impossible! And that three-hour stroll from table to stove? No, they, they and no one else, must pay me for that stroll! They must wash away that dishonor!"

"Faster!"

"And what if they take me to the police? Would they dare? They'd be afraid of a scandal. And what if Zverkov should refuse the duel out of contempt? That's even certain; but then I'll prove to them . . . Then I'll rush to the posting-house as he's leaving tomorrow, I'll grab him by the leg, I'll tear his overcoat off as he's getting into the coach. I'll fasten my teeth on his hand, I'll bite him. 'See, all of you, what a desperate man can be driven to!' Let him beat me on the head, and the rest of them from behind. I'll cry out to all the public: 'See, here's a young pup going off to charm the Circassian girls with my spit on his face!'

"After that, of course, everything's over! The department has vanished from the face of the earth. I'll be seized, I'll be taken to court, I'll be thrown out of work, put in prison, sent to Siberia, exiled. Who cares! Fifteen years later I'll drag myself after him, in rags, a beggar, when I'm let out of prison. I'll find him somewhere in a provincial capital. He'll be married and happy. He'll have a grown-up daughter . . . I'll say: 'Look, monster, look at my sunken cheeks and my rags! I lost everything—career, happiness, art, science, *a beloved woman—*

and all because of you. Here are the pistols. I've come to discharge my pistol, and . . . and I forgive you.' Here I'll fire into the air, and—no more will be heard of me . . ."

I even began to weep, though I knew perfectly well at the same moment that all this came from Silvio and from Lermontov's *Masquerade*.[15] And suddenly I felt terribly ashamed, so ashamed that I stopped the horse, got out of the sled, and stood in the snow in the middle of the street. The jack watched me with amazement and sighed.

What was to be done? To go there was impossible—the result would be nonsense; to leave things as they were was also impossible, because the result would then be . . . "Lord! How can I leave it! After such offenses! No!" I exclaimed, rushing back to the sled, "it's predestined, it's fate! Drive on, drive on—there!"

And in my impatience I hit the coachman in the neck with my fist.

"What's with you? Why're you punching?" the little peasant cried, lashing the nag, however, so that she started kicking with her hind legs.

Wet snow was falling in thick flakes; I uncovered myself, I didn't care about it. I forgot everything else, because I had finally resolved on the slap and felt with horror that it would happen *without fail now*, presently, and that *no power could stop it*. Desolate street-lamps flashed sullenly in the snowy haze, like torches at a funeral. Snow got under my overcoat, my jacket, my necktie, and melted there; I didn't cover myself; all was lost in any case! We drove up at last. I jumped out, almost unconscious, ran up the steps, and began knocking at the door with my hands and feet. My legs especially were growing weak, at the knees. The door was opened somehow quickly; as if they knew I was coming. (Indeed, Simonov had forewarned them that there might be one more, and they had to be forewarned there and generally to take precautions.

This was one of those "fashion shops" of the time, which have long since been done away with by the police. During the day it was actually a shop; and in the evening those who had references could come and visit.) I walked with quick steps through the dark store into the familiar drawing room, where only one candle was burning, and stopped in perplexity: no one was there.

"Where are they?" I asked someone.

But, of course, they had already had time to disperse . . .

In front of me stood a person with a stupid smile, the hostess herself, who knew me slightly. A moment later the door opened, and another person came in.

Paying no attention to anything, I was pacing the room and, I think, talking to myself. It was as if I had been saved from death, and I joyfully sensed it with my whole being: for I would have slapped him, I would certainly, certainly have slapped him! But now they're not here and . . . everything's vanished, everything's changed! . . . I kept looking over my shoulder. I still could not grasp it. Mechanically, I glanced at the girl who had come in: before me flashed a fresh, young, somewhat pale face, with straight dark eyebrows and serious, as if somewhat astonished, eyes. I liked it at once; I would have hated her if she'd been smiling. I began to study her more attentively and as if with effort: my thoughts were not all collected yet. There was something simple-hearted and kind in that face, yet somehow serious to the point of strangeness. I was certain that it was a disadvantage to her there, and that none of those fools had noticed her. However, she could not have been called a beauty, though she was tall, strong, well built. She was dressed extremely simply. Something nasty stung me; I went straight up to her . . .

By chance I looked in a mirror. My agitated face seemed to me repulsive in the extreme: pale, wicked, mean, with disheveled hair. "Let it be; I'm glad of it," I thought, "I'm precisely glad that I'll seem repulsive to her; I like it . . ."

VI

. . . Somewhere behind a partition, as if under some strong pressure, as if someone were strangling it, a clock wheezed. After an unnaturally prolonged wheeze, there followed a thin, vile, and somehow unexpectedly rapid chiming—as if someone had suddenly jumped forward. It struck two. I came to my senses, though I had not been asleep, but only lying there half-oblivious.

The room—narrow, small, and low, encumbered by a huge wardrobe, and littered with cartons, rags, and all sorts of cast-off clothing—was almost totally dark. The candle-butt burning on the table at the other end of the room was about to go out, barely flickering every now and then. In a few moments it would be quite dark.

It did not take me long to recover myself; everything came back to me at once, without effort, instantly, as if it had just been lying in wait to pounce on me again. And even in my oblivion there had still constantly remained some point, as it were, in my memory that simply refused to be forgotten, around which my drowsy reveries turned heavily. Yet it was strange: everything that had happened to me that day seemed to me now, on awakening, to have happened long, long ago, as if I had long, long ago outlived it all.

There were fumes in my head. Something was as if hovering over me, brushing against me, agitating and troubling me. Anguish and bile were again boiling up in me and seeking a way out. Suddenly I saw two open eyes beside me, peering at me curiously and obstinately. Their expression was coldly indifferent, sullen, as if utterly alien; it gave one a heavy feeling.

A sullen thought was born in my brain and passed through my whole body like some vile sensation, similar to what one feels on entering an underground cellar, damp and musty. It was somehow unnatural that these two eyes had only decided precisely now to begin peering at me. It also occurred to me that in the course of two hours I had not exchanged a single word with this being and had not considered it at all necessary; I had even liked it for some reason. But now, all of a sudden, there appeared before me the absurd, loathsomely spiderish notion of debauchery, which, without love, crudely and shamelessly begins straight off with that which is the crown of true love. We looked at each other like that for a long time, but she did not lower her eyes before mine, nor did she change their expression, and in the end, for some reason, this made me feel eerie.

"What's your name?" I asked curtly, so as to put a quick end to it.

"Liza," she replied, almost in a whisper, but somehow quite unpleasantly, and looked away.

I paused.

"The weather today . . . the snow . . . nasty!" I said, almost to myself, wearily putting my hand behind my head and looking at the ceiling.

She did not reply. The whole thing was hideous.

"Do you come from around here?" I asked after a minute, almost exasperated, turning my head slightly towards her.

"No."

"Where, then?"

"From Riga," she said reluctantly.

"German?"

"Russian."

"Been here long?"

"Where?"

"In this house."

"Two weeks." She spoke more and more curtly. The candle went out altogether; I could no longer make out her face.

"Do you have a father and mother?"

"Yes ... no ... I do."

"Where are they?"

"There ... in Riga."

"What are they?"

"Just ..."

"Just what? What are they, socially?"

"Tradespeople."

"You were living with them?"

"Yes."

"How old are you?"

"Twenty."

"Why did you leave them?"

"Just ..."

This "just" meant: let me alone, this is sickening. We fell silent.

God knows why I wouldn't leave. I myself felt more and more sickened and anguished. Images of the whole past day began to pass confusedly through my memory, somehow of themselves, without my will. I suddenly recalled a scene I had witnessed that morning in the street, as I was trotting along, preoccupied, to work.

"They were carrying a coffin out today and almost dropped it," I suddenly said aloud, not at all wishing to start a conversation, but just so, almost accidentally.

"A coffin?"

"Yes, in the Haymarket; they were carrying it out of a basement."

"Out of a basement?"

"Not a basement, but the basement floor . . . you know . . . down under . . . from a bad house . . . There was such filth all around . . . Eggshells, trash . . . stink . . . it was vile."

Silence.

"A bad day for a burial!" I began again, just not to be silent.

"Why bad?"

"Snow, slush . . ." (I yawned.)

"Makes no difference," she said suddenly, after some silence.

"No, it's nasty . . ." (I yawned again.) "The gravediggers must have been swearing because the snow was making it wet. And there must have been water in the grave."

"Why water in the grave?" she asked with a certain curiosity, but speaking even more rudely and curtly than before. Something suddenly began egging me on.

"There'd be water in the bottom for sure, about half a foot. Here in the Volkovo you can never dig a dry grave."

"Why not?"

"Why not? Such a watery place. It's swamp all around here. They just get put down in the water. I've seen it myself . . . many times . . ."

(I had never once seen it, and had never been in the Volkovo cemetery, but had only heard people talk.)

"It makes no difference to you how you die?"

"But why should I die?" she answered, as if defending herself.

"You'll die someday, and just the same way as that one today. She was also . . . a girl . . . She died of consumption."

"A jill would have died in the hospital . . ." (She already knows about that, I thought, and she said jill, not girl.)

"She owed money to the madam," I objected, egged on more and more by the argument, "and worked for her almost to the end, even though she had consumption. The cabbies around there were talking with the soldiers and told them about it. Probably her old acquaintances. They were laughing. They wanted to go and commemorate her in a pot-house." (Here, too, I was laying it on thick.)

Silence, deep silence. She did not even stir.

"So it's better to die in a hospital, is it?"

"What's the difference? . . . Anyway, who says I'm going to die?" she added irritably.

"If not now, then later?"

"Well, and later . . ."

"That's easy to say! You're young now, good-looking, fresh—so you're worth the price. But after a year of this life you won't be the same, you'll fade."

"In a year?"

"At any rate, in a year you'll be worth less," I went on, gloatingly. "So you'll go from here to somewhere lower, another house. A year later—to a third house, always lower and lower, and in about seven years you'll reach the Haymarket and the basement. That's still not so bad. Worse luck will be if on top of that some sickness comes along, say, some weakness of the chest . . . or you catch cold, or something. Sickness doesn't go away easily in such a life. Once it gets into you, it may not get out. And so you'll die."

"Well, so I'll die," she answered, very spitefully now, and stirred quickly.

"Still, it's a pity."

"For who?"

"A pity about life."

Silence.

"Did you have a fiancé? Eh?"

"What's it to you!"

"But I'm not questioning you. It's nothing to me. Why get angry? Of course, you may have had your own troubles. What's that to me? It's just a pity."

"For who?"

"For you."

"Don't bother . . ." she whispered, barely audibly, and stirred again.

This immediately fueled my anger even more. What! I was trying to be so gentle, and she . . .

"But what do you think? Is it a good path you're on, eh?"

"I don't think anything."

"And that's what's bad, that you don't think. Wake up while you have time. And you do have time. You're still young, good-looking; you could find love, marry, be happy . . ."

"Not all the married ones are happy," she snapped, in the same rude patter.

"Not all, of course—but even so it's much better than here. A whole lot better. And with love one can live even without happiness. Life is good even in sorrow, it's good to live in the world, no matter how. And what is there here except . . . stench. Phew!"

I turned to her with loathing; I was no longer reasoning coldly. I myself began to feel what I was saying, and became excited. I already thirsted to expound my cherished "little ideas," lived out in my corner. Something in me suddenly lit up, some goal "appeared."

"Never mind my being here, I'm no example for you. Maybe I'm even worse than you. Anyway, I was drunk when I stopped here," I still hastened to justify myself. "Besides, a man is no sort of example for a woman. It's a different thing; I may dirty and befoul myself, but all the same I'm nobody's slave; I'm here, then I'm gone, and that's all. I've shaken it off, and it's no longer me. But let's admit that you're a slave from the first beginning. Yes, a slave! You give up everything, all your will. Later you may want to break these chains, but no: they'll ensnare you more and more strongly. That's how this cursed chain is. I know it. I won't even speak about other things, you perhaps wouldn't understand me, but just tell me: no doubt you're already in debt to the madam? So, you see!" I added, though she did not answer me, but only listened silently, with her whole being; "there's a chain for you! Now you'll never get it paid off. That's how they do it. The same as selling your soul to the devil . . .

". . . Besides, I . . . how do you know, maybe I'm just as unfortunate as you are, and so I get into the muck on purpose, from misery. People do drink from grief: well, so I'm here—from grief. Now tell me, where's the good in it: here you and I . . . came together . . . tonight, and we didn't say a word to each other all the while, and only afterwards you started peering at me like a wild thing, and I at you. Is that any way to love? Is that any way for two human beings to come together? It's simply an outrage, that's what!"

"Yes!" she agreed, abruptly and hastily. I was even surprised by the hastiness of this "yes." So perhaps the same thought was wandering through her mind as she was peering at me just now? So she, too, is already capable of certain thoughts? . . . "Devil take it, that's curious, it's—*akin*," I reflected, almost rubbing my hands. "No, how can I fail to get the better of such a young soul? . . ."

It was the game that fascinated me most of all.

She turned her head closer to me and, it seemed to me in the darkness, propped it with her hand. Perhaps she was peering at me. How sorry I was that I couldn't make out her eyes. I heard her deep breathing.

"Why did you come here?" I began, now with a sense of power.

"I just . . ."

"And how good it would be to be living in your father's house! Warm, free; your own nest."

"And what if it's worse than that?"

A thought flashed in me: "I must find the right tone; sentimentality may not get me far."

However, it merely flashed. I swear she really did interest me. Besides, I was somehow unnerved and susceptible. And knavery goes so easily with feeling.

"Who can say!" I hastened to reply. "All sorts of things happen. Now, I'm sure someone wronged you, and it's rather they who are guilty before you than you before *them*. I know nothing of your story, but a girl of your sort certainly wouldn't come here of her own liking . . ."

"What sort of girl am I?" she whispered, barely audibly; but I heard it.

"Devil take it," I thought, "I'm flattering her. This is vile. Or maybe it's good . . ." She was silent.

"You see, Liza—I'll speak about myself! If I'd had a family in my childhood, I wouldn't be the same as I am now. I often think about it. No matter how bad things are in a family, still it's your father and mother, not enemies, not strangers. At least once a year they'll show love for you. Still you know you belong there. I grew up without a family: that must be why I turned out this way . . . unfeeling."

I bided my time again.

"Maybe she just doesn't understand," I thought, "and anyway it's ridiculous—this moralizing."

"If I were a father and had a daughter, I think I'd love my daughter more than my sons, really," I began obliquely, as if talking about something else, to divert her. I confess I was blushing.

"Why is that?" she asked.

Ah, so she's listening!

"I just would; I don't know, Liza. You see: I knew a father who was a stern, severe man, but he was forever on his knees before his daughter, kept kissing her hands and feet, couldn't have enough of admiring her, really. She'd be dancing at a party, and he'd stand for five hours in the same spot, unable to take his eyes off her. He was mad about her; I can understand that. She'd get tired at night and go to sleep, and he would wake up and start kissing her and making the sign of the cross over her while she slept. He himself went around in a greasy jacket, was niggardly with everybody, but for her he'd have spent his last kopeck, he kept giving her rich presents, and what a joy it was for him if she liked the present. A father always loves his daughters more than a mother does. It's a delight for some girls to live at home! And I don't think I'd even give my daughter in marriage."

"Why not?" she said, with a slight chuckle.

"I'd be jealous, by God. How could she kiss another man? Or love a stranger more than her father? It's even painful to imagine it. Of course, that's all nonsense; of course, everyone will finally see reason. But I think, before giving her away, I'd wear myself out just with worry: I'd reject one suitor after another. But in the end I'd marry her to the one she herself loved. To a father, the man his daughter falls in love with herself always seems the worst. That's how it is. Much harm is done in families because of it."

"Some are glad to sell their daughter, and not give her away honorably," she suddenly said.

Ah! That's what it is!

"That happens, Liza, in those cursed families where there is neither God nor love," I picked up heatedly, "and where there is no love, there is no reason. Such families do exist, it's true, but I'm not talking about them. Evidently you saw no goodness in your family, since you talk that way. You're one of the truly unfortunate ones. Hm . . . It all comes mainly from poverty."

"And is it any better with the masters? Honest people have good lives even in poverty."

"Hm . . . yes. Perhaps. Then there's this, Liza: man only likes counting his grief, he doesn't count his happiness. But if he were to count properly, he'd see that there's enough of both lots for him. Well, and what if everything goes right in the family, God blesses it, your husband turns out to be a good man, who loves you, pampers you, never leaves your side! It's good in this family! Oftentimes even half mixed with grief it's still good; and where is there no grief? Perhaps, once you get married, *you'll find out for yourself*. But take just the beginning, after you've married someone you love: there's such happiness at times, so much happiness! I mean, day in and day out. In the beginning, even quarrels with a husband end well. Some women, the more they love, the more they pick quarrels with their husbands. It's true; I knew such a woman: 'You see,' she all but said, 'I love you very much, and torment you out of love, and you ought to feel it.' Do you know that one can deliberately torment a person out of love? Women, mainly. And she thinks to herself: 'But afterwards I'll love him so much for it, I'll caress him so, that it's no sin to torment him a bit now.' And at home everyone rejoices over you, and it's good, and cheery, and peaceful, and honest . . . Then, too, there's the jealous sort. He goes out somewhere—I knew one like this—she can't help herself, she jumps out at night and runs on the sly to see: is he there, is he in that house, is he with that woman? Now, that is bad. And she knows herself that it's bad, and her heart is sinking, and she blames herself, and yet she loves him; it's all from love. And how good to make peace after a quarrel, to own up to him, or to forgive! And how good, how good they both suddenly feel—as if they were meeting anew, getting married anew, beginning to love anew. And no one, no one ought to know what goes on between a husband and wife if they love each other. And whatever quarrel they may have—they shouldn't call even their mother to be their judge or hear them tell about each other. They are their own judges. Love—is God's mystery, and should be hidden from all other eyes, whatever happens. It's holier that way, and better. They respect each other more, and so much is founded on respect. And if there was love once, if they were married out of love, why should love pass? Can't it be sustained? It rarely happens that it can't be. Well, and if the husband proves to be a kind and honest man, how can love pass? The first married love will pass, true, but then an even better love will come. Then their souls will grow close; they'll decide all their doings together; they'll have no secrets from each other. And when children arrive, then all of it, even the hardest times, will look like happiness; one need only love and have courage. Now even work brings joy, now even if you must occasionally deny yourself bread for the children's sake, still there is joy. For they will love you for it later; so you're laying aside for yourself. The children are growing—you feel you're an example to them, a support for them; that even when you die, they'll bear your thoughts and feelings upon themselves as they received them from you, they'll take on your image and likeness.[16] So it is a great duty. How can a father and mother fail to grow closer? People say it's hard having children. Who says so? It's a heavenly happiness! Do you love little children, Liza? I love them terribly. You know—there's this rosy little boy sucking at your breast, now what husband's heart could turn against his wife, looking at her sitting with his child! The baby is rosy, plump, pampered, sprawling; his little hands and feet are pudgy; his nails are so clean and small, so small it's funny to see; his eyes seem to understand everything already. He's sucking and clutching at your breast with his little hand, playing. The father comes up—he'll tear himself away from the breast, bend back, look at his father, laughing—as if it really were God knows how funny—and then again, again start sucking. Or else he'll up and bite his mother's breast, if he's already cutting teeth, while giving her a sidelong look: 'See how I bit you!' Isn't this the whole of happiness, when they're all three together, husband, wife, and child? A lot can be forgiven for those moments. No, Liza, one must first learn how to live, and only then accuse others!"

"With pictures," I thought to myself, "I'll get you with these pictures!"—though, by God, I had spoken with feeling—and suddenly blushed. "What if she suddenly bursts out laughing, what will I do with myself then?" The idea infuriated me. I had indeed become excited towards the end of my speech, and now my vanity somehow suffered. The silence continued. I even wanted to nudge her.

"It's like you . . ." she began suddenly, and stopped.

But I already understood everything: something different was trembling in her voice now, not sharp, not rude, not unyielding as before, but something soft and bashful, so bashful that I myself felt abashed, felt guilty before her.

"What?" I asked, with tender curiosity.

"But you . . ."

"What?"

"It's as if you . . . as if it's from a book," she said, and again something like mockery suddenly sounded in her voice.

I was painfully twinged by this remark. It was not what I was expecting.

I did not even understand that she was purposely assuming a mask of mockery, that this is the usual last device of a bashful and chaste-hearted person whose soul is being rudely and importunately pried into, and who will not surrender till the last minute out of pride, and is afraid of showing any feeling before you. I should have guessed it from the very timidity with which she ventured, haltingly, upon her mockery, before she finally brought herself to express it. But I did not guess, and a wicked feeling took hold of me.

"You just wait," I thought.

VII

"Eh, COME NOW, Liza, what have books got to do with it, if I myself feel vile for your sake. And not only for your sake. It all just rose up in my soul . . . Can it be, can it be that you don't find it vile here? No, habit evidently counts for a lot! Devil knows what habit can't make of a person. But can it be that you seriously think you'll never get old, that you'll be forever good-looking, and they'll keep you here forever and ever? It's foul enough even here, needless to say . . . However, this is what I can tell you about that, I mean, about your present life: granted you're young, attractive, nice, with a soul, with feelings; well, but do you know that when I came to my senses just now, I immediately felt vile for being here with you! One has to be drunk to end up here. But if you were in a different place, living as good people live, I might not just dangle after you, but simply fall in love with you, and be glad if you merely glanced at me, let alone spoke. I'd watch for you by the gate, I'd stay forever on my knees before you; I'd look upon you as my fiancée, and regard it as an honor. I wouldn't dare even think anything impure about you. While here I know I just have to whistle and, like it or not, you'll go with me, and it's no longer I who ask your will, but you mine. The merest peasant hires himself out to work—yet his bondage isn't total; besides, he knows there's a term to it. But where is your term? Just think: what is it you're giving up here? What are you putting in bondage? It's your soul, your soul, over which you have no power, that you put in bondage along with your body! You give your love to be profaned by any drunkard! Love!—but this is everything, it's a diamond, a maiden's treasure, this love! To deserve this love a man would be ready to lay down his soul, to face death. And what is the value of your love now? You're all bought, bought outright, and why try to obtain love if everything is possible without love? There's no worse offense for a girl, do you understand that? Now, I've heard that they humor you, fools that you are—they allow you to have lovers here. That's only an indulgence, only a deception, only a mockery of you, yet you believe it. What, does he really love you, this lover? I don't believe it. How can he love you, when he knows that you'll be called away from him any moment. He's a rotter in that case! Does he have even a drop of respect for you? What do you have in common with him? He's laughing at you while he steals from you—that's what his love amounts to! You can be thankful if he doesn't beat you. But maybe he does. Ask yours, if you have one: will he marry you? He'll burst out laughing in your face, if he doesn't spit, or give you a beating—and meanwhile his total worth is maybe two broken kopecks. And for the sake of what, one wonders, have you ruined your life here? For having coffee to drink, and being well fed? But what do they feed you for? Another woman, an honest one, would choke on it, because she'd know what they're feeding her for. You're in debt here, so you'll stay in debt, and you'll be in debt till the final end, till the time when the clients start spurning you. And that will come soon, don't count on your youth. It all flies by posthaste here. So they'll kick you out. And not simply kick you out, but first start picking on you long beforehand, reproaching you, abusing you—as if it wasn't you who gave her your health, destroyed your youth and soul for her in vain, but as if it was you who ruined her, beggared her, robbed her. And don't look for any support: the other girls will also attack you, to get in good with her, because everyone here is a slave and has long since lost all conscience and compassion. They're sunk in meanness, and no abuse in the world is more foul, mean, or offensive than that. And you'll lay down everything here, everything without stint—health, and youth, and beauty, and hopes—and at twenty-two you'll look like you're thirty-five, and you'll be lucky if you're not sick, pray to God for that. You must be thinking now that it's a picnic and not work at all! But there is not and never has been any harder or harsher work in the world than this. One would think your heart alone would simply pour itself out in tears. And you won't dare say a word, not half a word, when they throw you out of here; you'll go as if you were the one to blame. You'll go to another place, then to a third, then somewhere else, and finally you'll reach the Haymarket. And there they'll give you the routine beating; it's a courtesy of the place; there a client can't even be nice to a girl without beating her first. You don't believe it's so disgusting there? Go and look someday, maybe you'll see with your own eyes. I once saw a girl there, alone, by the door, on New Year's day. Her own people had kicked her out for the fun of it, to cool her off a bit, because she was howling too much, and locked the door behind her. At nine o'clock in the morning she was already completely drunk, disheveled, half-naked, all beaten up. Her face was powdered white, and her eyes were black-and-blue; blood was flowing from her nose and teeth: some coachman had just given her a pasting. She sat down on the stone stairs, holding some kind of salted fish; she was howling and wailing something about her 'miserble lot,' beating her fish against the steps. And coachmen and drunken soldiers crowded around the steps, teasing her. You don't believe you'll be the same? I wouldn't want to believe it either, but how do you know, maybe this same girl, the one with the salted fish, came here from somewhere ten or, say, eight years ago, fresh as a little cherub, innocent, pure, knowing no evil, and blushing at every word. Maybe she was just like you—proud, touchy, different from the rest; she had the look of a princess, and knew that complete happiness awaited the one who would love her, and whom she

would love. See where it ended up? And what if at the same
moment as she sat there, drunk and disheveled, beating her
fish on the dirty steps, what if at that moment she recalled all
her former pure years in her father's house, when she was still
going to school, and the neighbor's son used to watch for her
on the way, assured her he would love her all his life, that he
would make his fate hers, and they made a vow together to
love each other forever and to be married as soon as they got
bigger! No, Liza, it will be lucky, lucky for you if you die
quickly of consumption, someplace in a corner, in a basement,
like that girl. In a hospital, you say? If they take you there,
fine, but what if your madam still needs you? Consumption is
that sort of illness; it's not a fever. A person goes on hoping
till the last moment, saying he's well. It's just self-indulgence.
But there's profit in it for the madam. Don't worry, it's true;
you've sold your soul, you owe money besides, so you don't
dare make a peep. And when you're dying, they'll all abandon you, they'll all turn away from you—because what good
are you then? They'll even reproach you for uselessly taking
up space and not dying quickly enough. You'll have a hard
time getting a drink of water, they'll give it to you with a
curse: 'Hurry up and croak, you slut; you're moaning, people
can't sleep, the clients are disgusted.' It's true; I've overheard
such words myself. They'll shove you, on the point of croak-
ing, into the stinkingest corner of the basement—dark, damp;
what will you go over in your mind then, lying there alone?
You'll die—they'll lay you out hurriedly, strangers' hands,
grumblingly, impatiently—and no one will bless you, no one
will sigh over you, all they'll think is how to get you off their
backs quickly. They'll buy a pine box, take you out as they
did that poor girl today, and go to a pot-house to commemorate you. There's slush, muck, wet snow in the grave—they
won't go to any trouble over you. 'Lower her in, Vanyukha;
look at this "miserble lot" going legs up even here—the so-

and-so. Shorten the ropes, you rascal.' 'It'll do as it is.' 'What'll do? She's lying on her side. You got a human being here, don't you? Well, that'll do, fill it in.' They won't even want to argue long because of you. They'll cover you up quickly with wet blue clay and go to the pot-house ... That's the end of your memory on earth; other people's graves are visited by children, fathers, husbands, but at yours—not a tear, not a sigh, not a prayer, and no one, no one in the whole world will ever come to you; your name will disappear from the face of the earth—as if you'd never existed, as if you'd never been born! Mud and swamp, go ahead and knock on your coffin lid at night, when dead men rise: 'Let me out, good people, to live in the world! I lived—but saw nothing of life, my life was used up like an old rag; it got drunk up in a pot-house on the Haymarket; let me out, good people, to live in the world one more time! . . .' "

I waxed pathetic, so much so that I myself was about to have a spasm in my throat, when ... suddenly I stopped, raised myself in alarm, and, inclining my head fearfully, with pounding heart, began to listen. I indeed had reason to be troubled.

For a long time already I'd sensed that I had turned her whole soul over and broken her heart, and the more convinced of it I was, the more I wished to reach my goal quickly and as forcefully as possible. It was the game, the game that fascinated me; not just the game, however ...

I knew I'd been speaking stiffly, affectedly, even bookishly; in short, I couldn't speak any other way than "as if from a book." But that didn't trouble me; I knew, I sensed that I'd be understood, and that this very bookishness might even help things along. But now, having achieved my effect, I suddenly turned coward. No, never, never before had I witnessed such despair! She was lying prone, her face buried deep in her pillow, which she embraced with both arms. Her breast was bursting. Her whole young body was shuddering as in convulsions. Suppressed sobs were straining, tearing her breast, and would suddenly burst out in wails and cries. Then she'd cling to her pillow even more: she did not want anyone there, not a living soul, to learn of her torment and tears. She bit the pillow, she bit into her hand till it bled (I saw it later), or, clutching her loosened braids, she would go stiff with effort, holding her breath and clenching her teeth. I started to say something to her, to beg her to calm down, but felt I didn't dare, and suddenly, all in a sort of fever myself, almost horrified, I rushed gropingly, in haphazard haste, to get myself ready to go. It was dark: no matter how I tried, I couldn't finish quickly. Suddenly I touched a box of matches and a candlestick with a whole, unused candle. As soon as light shone in the room, Liza suddenly rose, sat up, and looked at me almost senselessly, with a somehow distorted face and a half-crazed smile. I sat down next to her and took her hands; she recovered herself, made a quick move as if to embrace me, but did not dare, and quietly bowed her head before me.

"Liza, my friend, I shouldn't have . . . forgive me," I tried to begin, but she squeezed my hands in her fingers with such force that I realized I was saying the wrong thing and stopped.

"Here's my address, Liza, come to me."

"I will . . ." she whispered resolutely, still without raising her head.

"And now I'll go, good-bye . . . till then."

I got up, she got up as well, and suddenly blushed all over, gave a start, grabbed a shawl that was lying on a chair, and wrapped her shoulders in it all the way to the chin. Having done so, she again smiled somehow painfully, blushed, and glanced at me strangely. I felt pained; I was in a hurry to leave, to efface myself.

"Wait," she said suddenly, already in the entryway and right at the door, stopping me with a hand on my overcoat, and in a flurry she set down the candle and ran off—she must have remembered something or wanted to bring something to show me. As she ran off, she blushed all over, her eyes shone, a smile appeared on her lips—what could it mean? Like it or not, I had to wait; she came back in a minute, her eyes as if apologizing for something. Generally, this was no longer the same face, the same look as before—sullen, mistrustful, and obstinate. Now her eyes were soft, pleading, and at the same time trustful, tender, timid. Children look that way at someone they love very much, when they're asking for something. She had light brown eyes, beautiful eyes, alive, capable of reflecting both love and sullen hatred.

Without explaining anything—as if, like some higher being, I must know everything without explanations—she handed me a piece of paper. Her whole face simply lit up at that moment with the most naive, childlike triumph. I unfolded it. It was a letter to her from some medical student or the like—a very grandiloquent, flowery, but extremely respectful declaration of love. I don't remember the expressions now, but I remember very well that through the high-flown style one caught glimpses of true feeling, which cannot be feigned. When I finished reading, I met her ardent, curious, and childishly impatient gaze on me. Her eyes were riveted to my face, and she waited impatiently—what would I say? In a few words, haphazardly, but somehow joyfully and as if proudly, she explained to me that she had been at a dancing party somewhere, in a family home, the home of some "very, very nice people, *family people*, and where *they still know nothing*, nothing at all," because she's still quite new here and just . . . and hasn't at all decided to stay yet, and will certainly leave as soon as she's paid her debt . . . "Well, and there was this student, dancing and talking with her all evening, and it turned out he had known her still in Riga, still as a child, they had played together, only very long ago—and he knew her parents, but he knows nothing, nothing, nothing *about this* and doesn't even suspect! And so, the next day after the dance (three days ago), he sent her this letter through a girlfriend with whom she'd gone to the party . . . and . . . well, that's all."

She lowered her flashing eyes somehow shyly as she finished telling me.

Poor little thing, she was keeping this student's letter as a treasure, and had run to fetch her only treasure, not wishing me to leave without knowing that she, too, was loved honestly and sincerely, that she, too, was spoken to respectfully. Most likely the letter was doomed simply to lie in a box without consequences. But what matter; I'm sure she would keep it all her life as a treasure, as her pride and justification, and now, at such a moment, she remembered the letter and brought it out to take naive pride before me, to restore herself in my eyes, so that I, too, should see, and I, too, should praise. I said nothing, pressed her hand, and walked out. I wanted so much to leave . . . I went the whole way on foot, in spite of the wet snow still falling in thick flakes. I was worn out, crushed, perplexed. But the truth was already shining through my perplexity. The nasty truth!

VIII

I<small>T TOOK ME</small> a while, however, to consent to recognize this truth. Having awakened in the morning after several hours of deep, leaden sleep, and having come at once to a realization of the whole day yesterday, I was even amazed at my yesterday's *sentimentality* with Liza, at all of "yesterday's horrors and pities." "Now there's a real fit of womanish nerves, pah!" I decided. "And why on earth did I shove my address at her? What if she comes? However, why not, let her come; it's no matter . . ." But, *obviously*, that was not the main and most important thing now: I had to make haste and, whatever the cost, quickly save my reputation in the eyes of Zverkov and Simonov. That was the main thing. And I even quite forgot about Liza that morning, what with all the bustle.

First of all, I had immediately to return yesterday's debt to Simonov. I resolved on a desperate measure: borrowing a whole fifteen roubles from Anton Antonovich. As luck would have it, he was in the most wonderful spirits that day, and handed me the money at once, at my first request. I was so glad that, as I signed the receipt, with a sort of bravado, I *casually* told him that yesterday I had done "a bit of carousing with some friends at the Hôtel de Paris; a farewell party for a schoolmate, even, one might say, a childhood friend—a big carouser, you know, a spoiled fellow—well, naturally, from a good family, a considerable fortune, a brilliant career, witty, charming, intrigues with all those ladies, you understand; we drank a 'half-dozen' too many, and . . ." And nothing to it; it was all spoken very lightly, easily, and smugly.

Having come home, I wrote at once to Simonov.

To this day I'm filled with admiration as I recall the truly gentlemanly, good-natured, frank tone of my letter. Adroitly, nobly, and, above all, with not a word too many—I blamed myself for everything. I excused myself, "if I may still be permitted to excuse myself," with being quite unaccustomed to wine, and thus becoming drunk at the first glass, which I (supposedly) drank before them, while waiting for them from five to six in the Hôtel de Paris. I mainly begged pardon of Simonov; and I asked him to convey my explanations to all the others, especially Zverkov, whom, "I recall as in a dream," I seemed to have insulted. I added that I would have gone to them all myself, but I had a headache and, above all, was ashamed. I remained especially pleased with the "certain lightness," even all but casual (though perfectly decent), that suddenly reflected itself in my pen and at once gave them to understand, better than any possible reasons, that I looked upon "all that nastiness yesterday" quite independently; in no way, by no means, was I killed on the spot, as you good sirs probably think, but on the contrary I looked upon it as befits a calmly self-respecting gentleman. "The errors of youth are soon forgotten," as they say.

"And that certain marquisian playfulness, even?" I admired, rereading the note. "And all because I'm a developed and educated man! Others in my place wouldn't know how to extricate themselves, and here I've wriggled out of it and can go on carousing, and all because I'm 'an educated and developed man of our times.' Besides, maybe it really did all come from the wine yesterday. Hm . . . well, no, not from the wine. And I didn't drink any vodka between five and six, while I was waiting for them. I lied to Simonov; lied shamelessly; and even now I'm not ashamed . . .

"Ah, spit on it, however! I'm out of it, that's the main thing."

I put six roubles into the letter, sealed it, and prevailed upon Apollon to take it to Simonov. On learning that there was money inside, Apollon became more respectful and agreed to go. Towards evening I went out for a stroll. My head was still aching and dizzy from yesterday. But the more evening advanced and the twilight thickened, the more my impressions and, after them, my thoughts as well, kept changing and tangling. Something within me, deep in my heart and conscience, would not die, refused to die, and betrayed itself in a burning anguish. I loitered about mainly on the most crowded business streets—Meshchanskaya, Sadovaya, around the Yusupov Garden. I had always liked especially to stroll along those streets at twilight, precisely when the crowd thickens with all sorts of passers-by, merchants, and tradesmen, their faces preoccupied to the point of anger, going home from their daily work. I precisely liked this twopenny bustle, this insolent prosiness. But now all this street jostling only irritated me the more. I simply could not get hold of myself, could not find the loose ends. Something in my soul was rising, rising, ceaselessly, painfully, and refused to be still. I returned home thoroughly upset. Like as if some crime lay on my soul.

I was constantly tormented by the thought that Liza would come. What I found strange was that, of all those memories from yesterday, the memory of her tormented me somehow specially, somehow quite separately. By evening I had already quite successfully forgotten all the rest, brushed it aside, and I was still perfectly pleased with my letter to Simonov. But with this I was somehow not so pleased. It was like as if I were tormented over Liza alone. "What if she comes?" I thought ceaselessly. "Well, no matter, let her come. Hm. The only bad thing is that she'll see, for example, how I live. Yesterday I showed myself to her as such a . . . hero . . . and now, hm! It's bad, however, that I've gone so much to seed. Sheer poverty in the apartment. And I dared go to dinner yesterday in such clothes! And this oilcloth sofa of mine, with the stuffing hanging out of it! And this dressing gown that doesn't even cover me! Such tatters . . . And she'll see all this; and she'll see Apollon. The brute is sure to insult her. He'll pick on her in order to be rude to me. And I, of course, as is my custom, will turn coward, start mincing before her, covering myself with the skirts of my dressing gown, start smiling, start lying. Ohh, vileness! And that's not even the chief vileness! There's something chiefer in it, viler, meaner! Yes, meaner! And again, again to put on that dishonorable, lying mask! . . ."

Having arrived at this thought, I simply flared up:

"Why dishonorable? What's dishonorable? I spoke sincerely yesterday. I remember there was also true feeling in me. I precisely wanted to evoke noble feelings in her . . . if she cried a bit, that's good, it'll have a good effect . . ."

But all the same I just could not calm down.

That whole evening, when I'd already returned home, when it was already past nine and by my reckoning Liza simply could not come, I still kept imagining her, and I recalled her, mostly, in one and the same position. Namely, of all that had happened yesterday, I pictured one moment especially vividly: it was when I lighted up the room with a match and saw her pale, distorted face with its tormented eyes. And how pathetic, how unnatural, how twisted her smile was at that moment! But I did not know then that even after fifteen years I would still be picturing Liza precisely with the pathetic, twisted, needless smile she had at that moment.

The next day I was again prepared to regard it all as nonsense, frazzled nerves, and, above all—*exaggeration*. I was always aware of this weak link in me, and at times was very afraid of it: "I'm forever exaggerating; that's where I'm lame," I repeated to myself at all hours. But nevertheless, "nevertheless, Liza may still come"—this was the refrain with which all my reasonings at that time concluded. I worried so much that I sometimes became furious. "She'll come! She's sure to come!" I'd exclaim, running up and down my room. "If not today, then tomorrow, but she'll find me! That's the cursed romanticism of all these *pure hearts*! Oh, the vileness, oh, the stupidity, oh, the narrowness of these 'rotten, sentimental souls'! How can one not understand, how indeed can one not understand? . . ." But here I myself would stop, and even in great confusion.

"And it took so little, so little talk," I thought in passing, "such a little idyll (an affected idyll besides, a contrived, a bookish one), to succeed in turning a whole human soul the way I wanted. There's virginity for you! There's the freshness of the soil!"

At times the thought occurred to me of going to her myself, "to tell her everything" and prevail upon her not to come to me. But here, at this thought, such spite rose up in me that

I think I would simply have squashed this "cursed" Liza if she'd suddenly happened to be there, insulted her, spat upon her, driven her out, struck her!

A day passed, however, then another, then a third—she did not come, and I began to calm down. I especially took heart and let myself go after nine o'clock, I sometimes even began to dream, and that quite sweetly: "I save Liza," for example, "precisely through her coming to me, and my telling her . . . I develop her, educate her. I finally notice that she loves me, loves me passionately. I pretend not to understand (I don't know, however, why I pretend; probably just for the beauty of it). At last, all confused, beautiful, trembling and weeping, she throws herself at my feet and says that I am her savior, and that she loves me more than anything in the world. I am amazed, but . . . 'Liza,' I say, 'can you really think I haven't noticed your love? I saw everything, I guessed, but I dared not presume first upon your heart, because I had influence over you and feared lest you, out of gratitude, might deliberately make yourself return my love, might call up by force a feeling that perhaps is not there, and I did not want that, because that is . . . despotism . . . It is indelicate' " (well, in short, here I let my tongue run away with me in some such European, George-Sandian, ineffably noble refinement . . .).[17]
" 'But now, now—you are mine, you are my creation, you are pure, beautiful, you are—my beautiful wife.

> 'And now, full mistress of the place,
> Come bold and free into my house.'[18]

"And then we begin living happily ever after, go abroad, etc., etc." In short, I felt vile and would end by sticking my tongue out at myself.

"They won't even let the 'slut' come!" I thought. "They don't seem to allow them out much, especially in the evening" (for some reason it seemed certain to me that she must come in the evening, and precisely at seven o'clock). "Though she said she's not completely bound to them yet, she has some special privileges there; so—hm! Devil take it, she'll come, she's sure to come!"

It was a good thing Apollon diverted me at that time with his rudeness. Drove me out of all patience! He was my thorn, a scourge visited upon me by Providence. He and I had been in constant altercation for several years on end, and I hated him. My God, how I hated him! I think I've never in my life hated anyone as I did him, especially at certain moments. He was an elderly, imposing man, who occupied himself part of the time with tailoring. I don't know why, but he despised me even beyond all measure and looked at me with an insufferable haughtiness. But then he looked at everyone with haughtiness. One glance at that pale-haired, slicked-down head, at the quiff he fluffed up on his forehead and oiled with vegetable oil, at that serious mouth forever pursed in a V— and you immediately sensed before you a being who never doubted himself. He was in the highest degree a pedant, and the most enormous pedant of any I've ever met on earth; and this was accompanied by a vanity perhaps befitting only Alexander of Macedon. He was in love with his every button, his every fingernail—absolutely in love, and he looked it! He treated me quite despotically, spoke extremely little with me, and if he chanced to let his eyes rest on me, he did so with a firm, majestically self-confident, and permanently mocking look, which sometimes drove me to fury. He fulfilled his duties with such an air as if he were bestowing the highest favor upon me. However, he did almost exactly nothing for me, and did not even consider himself obliged to do anything. There was no doubting that he considered me the most complete fool in the whole world, and if he "kept me around," it was solely because he could get his wages from me every month. He agreed to "do nothing" in my service for seven roubles a month. Many sins will be forgiven me for him. It sometimes reached such hatred that I'd be all but thrown into convulsions by his gait alone. But I loathed his lisp especially. His tongue was a bit longer than it should have been, or something like that, which caused him to be forever lisping and sissing, and he was apparently terribly proud of it, imagining that it lent him a great deal of dignity. He spoke softly, measuredly, placing his hands behind his back and looking down. He especially infuriated me when he'd start reading the Psalter behind his partition. I endured many a battle on account of that reading. But he liked terribly much to read in the evenings, in a soft, even voice, chanting as over a dead body. Curiously, that's how he ended up: he now hires himself out to read the Psalter over the deceased, and along with that he exterminates rats and makes shoe polish. But at the time I was unable to throw him out, as though he had combined chemically with my existence. Besides, he would not have agreed to leave me for anything. It was impossible for me to live in *chambres garnies*:¹⁹ my apartment was my mansion, my shell, my case, in which I hid from all mankind, and Apollon, it seemed to me—devil knows why—belonged to that apartment, and for a whole seven years I was unable to throw him out.

To withhold his wages, for example, for as little as two or three days, was impossible. He'd make such a to-do that I wouldn't even know where to hide. But in those days I was so embittered against everyone that I resolved, who knows why or what for, to *punish* Apollon and not give him his wages for another two weeks. I had long been intending to do this, for two years or so—solely to prove to him that he dared not get so puffed up over me, and that if I wished I could always not give him his wages. I decided not to tell him about it and even to maintain a deliberate silence, in order to vanquish his pride and make him be the first to speak of his wages. Then I would take all seven roubles from the drawer, to show him that I had them and had deliberately set them aside, but that I "did not, did not, simply did not want to give him his wages, did not want to because *that's how I wanted it*, because such was 'my will as the master,' because he was irreverent, because he was a boor; but that if he asked reverently, perhaps I would relent and pay him; otherwise he'd have to wait another two weeks, wait three weeks, wait a whole month . . ."

But, angry though I was, the victory still went to him. I didn't even hold out for four days. He began with what he always began with on such occasions—for there had already been such occasions, or attempts (and, I will note, I knew it all beforehand, I knew his mean tactics by heart)—that is, he usually began by fixing me with an extremely stern look, not taking it off me for several minutes at a time, following me with his eyes especially when I came in or was leaving the house. If, for example, I held out and pretended not to notice these looks, he would proceed, silently as ever, to further tortures. Suddenly, for no reason at all, he would come softly and smoothly into my room while I was pacing about or reading, stop by the door, put one arm behind his back, thrust out one hip, and fix me with his eyes, no longer so much stern as altogether contemptuous. If I suddenly asked him what he wanted, he would make no reply, and go on staring at me point-blank for several seconds more; then, pressing his lips together in some special way, with a significant air, he would turn slowly on his heel and suddenly go to his room. About two hours later he would suddenly emerge again, and again appear before me in the same way. Sometimes, in my fury, I would no longer ask what he wanted, but simply raise my head abruptly and imperiously, and also begin staring point-blank at him. And so we'd stare at each other like that for about two minutes; finally, he would turn, slowly and pompously, and go away for another two hours.

If I refused to be brought to reason by all this and continued my rebellion, he would suddenly begin to sigh as he looked at me, sigh long and deeply, as if measuring with each sigh the full depth of my moral fall, and, of course, it would end at last with him overcoming me completely: I'd get furious, I'd shout, but with that which had been the whole point I'd be forced to comply.

This time, however, as soon as the usual "stern look" maneuvers began, I immediately lost my temper and fell on him in a fury. I was all too irritated to begin with.

"Stop!" I yelled in a frenzy, as he was turning, slowly and silently, one arm behind his back, to go to his room. "Stop! Come back! Come back, I tell you!" And I must have bellowed so unnaturally that he turned and began to study me even with a certain surprise. However, he still did not say a word, and it was this that infuriated me.

"How dare you come in here without permission and stare at me like that! Answer!"

But he, having looked at me calmly for about half a minute, again began to turn around.

"Stop!" I roared, running up to him, "don't move! So. Now answer: what did you come in here and stare for?"

"If there's something you want done direckly, it's my duty to see to it," he replied, again after some silence, lisping softly and measuredly, raising his eyebrows, and calmly shifting his head from one side to the other—and all that with horrifying composure.

"That's not it, that's not what I'm asking you, hangman!" I shouted, shaking with anger. "I'll tell you myself, hangman, why you keep coming here: you see I'm not giving you your wages, in your pride you don't want to bow and beg, and for that you come with your stupid staring to punish me, to torture me, and you don't even r-r-realize, hangman, how stupid it is, stupid, stupid, stupid, stupid!"

He again began to turn silently, but I grabbed him.

"Listen," I was shouting at him. "Here's the money, see, here it is!" (I took it out of the drawer.) "All seven roubles, but you won't get it, you will not get it, until such time as you come respectfully, with a guilty head, to ask my forgiveness. Do you hear!"

"That can never be!" he replied, with a sort of unnatural self-assurance.

"It will be!" I was shouting. "I give you my word of honor, it will be!"

"And there's nothing for me to ask your forgiveness about," he went on, as if not noticing my shouts at all, "seeing as you yourself have abused me with 'hangman,' on which offense I can always apply against you at the precinct."

"Go! Apply!" I roared. "Go now, this minute, this second! And you're still a hangman! hangman! hangman!" But he just looked at me, then turned and, no longer listening to my appeals, went smoothly to his place without a backward glance.

"There wouldn't be any of this if it weren't for Liza!" I decided to myself. Then, after a moment's pause, pompously and solemnly, but slowly and with a pounding heart, I myself proceeded behind his screen.

"Apollon!" I said softly and measuredly, though I was suffocating, "go for the police chief at once, without the slightest delay!"

He had managed meanwhile to sit down at his table, put on his spectacles, and begin some sewing. But hearing my order, he suddenly snorted with laughter.

"Go now, this minute! Go, or you can't even imagine what will happen!"

"Truly, you're not in your right senses," he observed, without even raising his head, with the same slow lisp, and continuing to thread his needle. "Who's ever seen a man go to the authorities against himself? And as to scaring me—you're exerting yourself in vain, because—nothing will happen."

"Go!" I shrieked, grabbing him by the shoulder. I felt I was about to strike him.

And I did not even hear how the outer door opened at that moment, softly and slowly, and some figure entered, stopped, and began gazing at us in perplexity. I looked, died of shame, and rushed to my room. There, clutching my hair with both hands, I leaned my head against the wall and stood frozen in that position.

About two minutes later I heard the slow steps of Apollon.

"*Some . . . one* is asking for you out there," he said, looking at me with particular sternness, then stepped aside and let in— Liza. He did not want to leave, and stared at us mockingly.

"Get out! Get out!" I ordered repeatedly, quite lost. At that moment my clock strained, hissed, and struck seven.

IX

And now, full mistress of the place,
Come bold and free into my house.
From the same poetry

I STOOD before her, destroyed, branded, disgustingly embarrassed, and, I think, smiling, trying as hard as I could to wrap myself in my ragged old quilted dressing gown—well, exactly as I had pictured to myself recently in fallen spirits. Apollon hovered around us for about two minutes and then left, but that made it no easier for me. Worst of all was that she, too, suddenly became embarrassed, much more so than I would even have expected. From looking at me, of course.

"Sit down," I said mechanically, and moved a chair out for her at the table, while I myself sat on the sofa. She sat down at once and obediently, staring at me all eyes, apparently expecting something from me right then. The naivety of this expectation infuriated me, but I restrained myself.

The thing to do here would have been to try not to notice anything, as if it were all quite ordinary, but she . . . And I sensed vaguely that she was going to pay dearly *for it all* . . .

"You find me in an odd situation, Liza," I began, stammering, and knowing that this was precisely not how I should have begun.

"No, no, don't think anything of the sort!" I cried, seeing her suddenly blush. "I'm not ashamed of my poverty . . . On the contrary, I look upon my poverty with pride. I'm poor, but noble . . . One can be poor and noble," I went on mumbling. "However . . . would you like some tea?"

"No . . ." she tried to begin.

"Wait!"

I jumped up and ran to Apollon. I really had to vanish somewhere.

"Apollon," I whispered in a feverish patter, flinging down before him the seven roubles, which had remained in my fist all the while, "here's your wages; see, I'm giving it to you; but for that you must save me: go at once and bring some tea and ten rusks from the tavern. If you refuse to go, you'll ruin a man's happiness. You don't know what this woman is . . . This is—everything. You're perhaps having certain thoughts . . . But you don't know what this woman is! . . ."

Apollon, who had already sat down to work, and had already put his spectacles back on, at first, without abandoning his needle, silently cast a sidelong glance at the money; then, paying no attention to me and not answering me at all, he went on fussing with his thread, which he was still trying to put through the needle. I waited for about three minutes, standing before him, my arms folded à la Napoleon. My temples were damp with sweat; I was pale, I could sense it. But, thank God, he must have felt sorry looking at me. Having finished with his needle, he slowly rose from his seat, slowly moved the chair aside, slowly took off his spectacles, slowly counted the money, and at last, having asked me over his shoulder: should he get a full portion?—slowly walked out of the room. As I was returning to Liza, it occurred to me on the way: why don't I flee, just as I am, in my wretched old dressing gown, wherever my feet take me, and come what may?

I sat down again. She looked at me anxiously. For several minutes we said nothing.

"I'll kill him!" I suddenly cried, banging my fist so hard on the table that the ink splashed out of the inkstand.

"Ah! What is it!" she cried with a start.

"I'll kill him, I'll kill him!" I was shrieking, pounding on the table, in a perfect frenzy, and at the same time with a perfect understanding of how stupid it was to be in such a frenzy.

"You don't know, Liza, what this hangman is for me. He's my hangman . . . He's just gone to get some rusks; he . . ."

And I suddenly broke down in tears. It was a fit. Oh, how ashamed I was between sobs; but I could no longer hold them back.

She was frightened. "What is it! What's the matter!" she kept crying out, bustling around me.

"Water, give me water, over there!" I murmured in a weak voice, conscious, however, within myself, that I was quite well able to do without water and not to murmur in a weak voice. But I was *putting on a show*, as they say, to preserve decency, though the fit was a real one.

She gave me water, looking at me as if lost. At that moment Apollon brought in the tea. It suddenly seemed to me that this ordinary and prosaic tea was terribly indecent and measly after all that had happened, and I blushed. Liza looked at Apollon even fearfully. He went out without glancing at us.

"Liza, do you despise me?" I said, looking at her point-blank, trembling with impatience to find out what she thought.

She became embarrassed, and was unable to reply.

"Drink your tea!" I said spitefully. I was angry with myself, but, naturally, she was going to bear the brunt of it. A terrible spite against her suddenly boiled up in my heart; I think I could simply have killed her. To be revenged on her, I swore mentally not to speak even one word to her from then on. "It's she who caused it all," I thought.

Our silence had already lasted some five minutes. The tea sat on the table; we didn't touch it: it went so far that I purposely refused to begin drinking, so as to make it still harder for her; and it would have been awkward for her to begin. Several times she glanced at me in sad perplexity. I was stubbornly silent. The chief martyr, of course, was myself, because I was fully conscious of all the loathsome baseness of my spiteful stupidity, and at the same time I simply could not restrain myself.

"I want . . . to get out of there . . . for good," she tried to begin, in order to break the silence somehow, but, poor thing! she precisely ought not to have started with that at such a moment, stupid as it was to begin with, or to such a man, stupid as I was to begin with. Even my heart ached from pity for her ineptness and unnecessary candor. But something ugly immediately suppressed all pity in me; it even egged me on still more: perish the whole world! Another five minutes passed.

"Perhaps I've disturbed you?" she began timidly, in a barely audible voice, and started to get up.

But as soon as I saw this first flash of injured dignity I simply trembled with anger and at once burst out.

"What did you come to me for, do tell me, please?" I began, suffocating, and not even considering the logical order of my words. I wanted to speak everything out at once, in one shot; I didn't even care where I began.

"Why did you come? Answer! Answer!" I kept exclaiming, all but beside myself. "I'll tell you why you came, my dear. You came because of the *pathetic words* I used with you then. So you went all soft, and you wanted more 'pathetic words.' Know, then, know that I was laughing at you that time. And I'm laughing now. Why do you tremble? Yes, laughing! I'd been insulted earlier, at dinner, by the ones who came there ahead of me. I came there to give a thrashing to one of them, the officer; but I didn't succeed, he wasn't there; I needed to unload my offense on someone, to get my own back, and you turned up, so I poured out my spite and laughed at you. I'd been humiliated, so I, too, wanted to humiliate; they'd ground me down like a rag, so I, too, wanted to show my power . . . That's what it was, and you thought I came then on purpose to save you, right? That's what you thought? That's what you thought?"

I knew she might perhaps get confused and not understand the details; but I also knew she'd understand the essence perfectly well. And so it happened. She turned white as a sheet, tried to utter something, her mouth twisted painfully; but, as if cut down with an axe, she sank onto the chair. And all the rest of the time she listened to me with open mouth, with wide open eyes, and trembling in terrible fear. The cynicism, the cynicism of my words crushed her . . .

"To save you!" I went on, jumping up from my chair and running back and forth in front of her, "to save you from what! But maybe I'm worse than you are. Why didn't you fling it in my mug when I started reading you my oration: 'And you, what did you come here for? To teach us morals, or what?' Power, power, that's what I wanted then, the game was what I wanted, I wanted to achieve your tears, your humiliation, your hysterics—that's what I wanted then! But I couldn't stand it myself, because I'm trash, I got all scared and, like a fool, gave you my address, devil knows why. And afterwards, even before I got home, I was already cursing you up and down for that address. I already hated you, because I'd lied to you then. Because I only talk a good game, I only dream in my head, but do you know what I want in reality? That you all go to hell, that's what! I want peace. I'd sell the whole world for a kopeck this minute, just not to be bothered. Shall the world go to hell, or shall I not have my tea? I say let the world go to hell, but I should always have my tea. Did you know that or not? Well, and I do know that I'm a black-guard, a scoundrel, a self-lover, a lazybones. I spent these past three days trembling for fear you might come. And do you know what particularly bothered me all these three days? That I had presented myself to you as such a hero then, and now you'd suddenly see me in this torn old dressing gown, abject, vile. I just told you I was not ashamed of my poverty; know, then, that I am ashamed, I'm ashamed of it most of all, afraid of it more than anything, more than of being a thief, because I'm so vain it's as if I'd been flayed and the very air hurts me. But can you possibly not have realized even now that I will never forgive you for having found me in this wretched dressing gown, as I was hurling myself like a vicious little cur at Apollon? The resurrector, the former hero, fling-ing himself like a mangy, shaggy mutt at his lackey, who just laughs at him! And those tears a moment ago, which, like an ashamed woman, I couldn't hold back before you, I will never forgive you! And what I'm confessing to you now, I will also never forgive *you*! Yes—you, you alone must answer for all this, because you turned up here, because I'm a scoundrel, because I'm the most vile, the most ridiculous, the most petty, the most stupid, the most envious of all worms on earth, who are in no way better than I, but who, devil knows why, are never embarrassed; while I will just go on being flicked all my life by every nit—that's my trait! Besides, what do I care if you won't understand a word of it! And what, tell me, what, what do I care about you and whether you're perishing there or not? Do you understand, now that I've spoken it all out to you, how I'm going to hate you for being here and listening? Because a man speaks out like this only once in his life, and then only in hysterics! ... What more do you want? Why, after all this, do you still stick there in front of me, tormenting me, refusing to leave?"

But here a strange circumstance suddenly occurred.

I was so used to thinking and imagining everything from books, and to picturing everything in the world to myself as I had devised it beforehand in my dreams, that at first I didn't even understand this strange circumstance. What occurred was this: Liza, whom I had insulted and crushed, understood far more than I imagined. She understood from it all what a woman, if she loves sincerely, always understands before anything else—namely, that I myself was unhappy.

The frightened and insulted feeling in her face first gave way to rueful amazement. And when I began calling myself a scoundrel and a blackguard, and my tears poured down (I had spoken the entire tirade in tears), her whole face twisted in a sort of convulsion. She wanted to get up, to stop me; and when I came to the end, she paid no attention to my cries: "Why are you here, why don't you leave!" but only to how very hard it must have been for me to speak it all out. Besides, she was so downtrodden, poor thing; she considered herself infinitely beneath me; how could she be angry or offended? She suddenly jumped from her chair on some irrepressible impulse, and, all yearning towards me, but still timidly, not daring to move from the spot, stretched out her arms to me ... Here my heart, too, turned over in me. Then she suddenly rushed to me, threw her arms about my neck, and burst into tears. I, too, could not help myself and broke into such sobbing as had never happened to me before ...

"They won't let me ... I can't be ... good!" I barely articulated, then went to the sofa, fell face down, and sobbed for a quarter of an hour in real hysterics. She leaned towards me, embraced me, and remained as if frozen in that embrace.

But still, the hitch was that the hysterics did have to end. And so (I am writing the loathsome truth), lying prone on the sofa, my face buried hard in the wretched leather cushion, I began little by little, remotely, involuntarily, but irresistibly, to feel that it would be awkward now to raise my head and look straight into Liza's eyes. What was I ashamed of? I don't know, but I was ashamed. It also came into my agitated head that the roles were now finally reversed, that she was now the heroine, and I was the same crushed and humiliated creature as she had been before me that night—four days ago . . . And all this came to me during those minutes when I was still lying prone on the sofa!

My God! but can it be that I envied her then?

I don't know, to this day I cannot decide, and then, of course, I was even less able to understand it than now. For without power and tyranny over someone, I really cannot live . . . But . . . but reasoning explains nothing, and consequently there's no point in reasoning.

I mastered myself, however, and raised my head; indeed, I had to raise it sometime . . . And then—I am convinced of it even to this day—precisely because I was ashamed to look at her, another feeling suddenly kindled and flared up in my heart . . . the feeling of domination and possession. My eyes gleamed with passion, and I squeezed her hands hard. How I hated her and how drawn I was to her at that moment! One feeling intensified the other. This was almost like revenge! . . . At first, a look as if of perplexity, even as if of fear, came to her face, but only for a moment. She embraced me rapturously and ardently.

X

A QUARTER OF an hour later I was running up and down my room in furious impatience, going to the screen every other minute and peeking at Liza through a crack. She was sitting on the floor, her head leaning against the bed, and was probably crying. But she wouldn't leave, and that was what irritated me. This time she knew everything. I had given her the final insult, but . . . no use talking about it. She guessed that my burst of passion was precisely revenge, a new humiliation for her, and that to my previous, almost pointless hatred there had now been added a *personal, envious* hatred of her . . . I do not insist, by the way, that she understood it all clearly; but on the other hand she fully understood that I was a loathsome man and, above all, incapable of loving her.

I know I shall be told that all this is inconceivable, that it is inconceivable to be as wicked, as stupid, as I was; perhaps it will also be added that it was inconceivable not to love her, or at least not to appreciate her love. But why inconceivable? First, I was no longer able to love, because, I repeat, for me to love meant to tyrannize and to preponderize morally. All my life I've been incapable even of picturing any other love, and I've reached the point now of sometimes thinking that love consists precisely in the right, voluntarily granted by the beloved object, to be tyrannized over. In my underground dreams as well, I never pictured love to myself otherwise than as a struggle; for me it always started from hatred and ended with moral subjugation, and afterwards I couldn't even picture to myself what to do with the subjugated object. And how is it inconceivable, if I had managed so to corrupt myself morally, had grown so unaccustomed to "living life," that I had dared just before to reproach and shame her for coming to me to hear "pathetic words"; and I myself never guessed that she had come to me not at all to hear pathetic words, but to love me, because for a woman it is in love that all resurrection, all salvation from ruin of whatever sort, and all regeneration consists, nor can it reveal itself in anything else but this. However, I did not hate her all that much as I was running about my room and peeking behind the screen through a crack. I simply felt it unbearably burdensome that she was there. I wanted her to disappear. I longed for "peace," I longed to be left alone in the underground. "Living life" so crushed me, unaccustomed to it as I was, that it even became difficult for me to breathe.

But several more minutes passed and she still did not get up, as if she were oblivious. I was shameless enough to tap softly on the screen to remind her . . . She suddenly roused herself, started up from her place, and rushed to look for her scarf, her hat, her fur coat, as if to escape from me somewhere . . . Two minutes later she came slowly from behind the screen and gave me a heavy look. I grinned spitefully, though forcedly, *for decency's sake*, and turned away from her look.

"Good-bye," she said, making for the door.

I suddenly ran to her, seized her hand, opened it, put . . . and closed it again. Then I turned at once and quickly sprang away to the opposite corner, so as at least not to see . . .

I was going to lie right now—to write that I did it accidentally, in distraction, at a loss, out of foolishness. But I don't want to lie, and so I'll say directly that I opened her hand and put . . . in it out of malice. The thought of doing it occurred to me while I was running up and down my room and she was sitting behind the screen. But this much I can say with certainty: although I did this cruelty on purpose, it came not from my heart, but from my stupid head. This cruelty was so affected, so much from the head, so purposely contrived, so *bookish*, that I myself could not bear it even for a minute—first I sprang away to the corner so as not to see, then in shame and despair I rushed after Liza. I opened the door to the landing and began to listen.

"Liza! Liza!" I called out to the stairway, but timidly, in a low voice . . .

There was no answer; I thought I could hear her footsteps down below.

"Liza!" I called more loudly.

No answer. But at that moment I heard from below the tight glass outer door to the street creak open heavily and slam tightly shut again. The bang echoed up the stairway.

She was gone. I went back to my room, pondering. I felt terribly heavy.

I stopped by the table next to the chair on which she had been sitting, and stared senselessly before me. About a minute passed; suddenly I gave a great start: there before me, on the table, I saw . . . in short, I saw a crumpled blue five-rouble bill, the very one I had pressed into her hand a moment before. It was *that* bill; it couldn't have been any other; there wasn't any other in the house. So she had managed to fling it from her hand onto the table just as I jumped away to the opposite corner.

Well, then? I could have expected her to do that. Could have expected? No. I was so great an egoist, I had in fact so little respect for people, that I could scarcely imagine she, too, would do that. I couldn't bear it. A second later I rushed like a madman to get dressed, threw on in a flurry whatever I could find, and raced headlong after her. She couldn't have gone more than two hundred steps before I ran out to the street.

It was still, and the snow was falling heavily, almost perpendicularly, laying a pillow over the sidewalk and the deserted roadway. Not a single passer-by, not a sound to be heard. The street-lamps flickered glumly and uselessly. I ran about two hundred steps to the intersection and stopped.

"Where did she go? And why am I running after her? Why? To fall down before her, to weep in repentance, to kiss her feet, to beg forgiveness! I wanted it; my whole breast was tearing apart, and never, never will I recall this moment with indifference. But—why?" came the thought. "Won't I hate her, maybe tomorrow even, precisely for kissing her feet today? Will I bring her happiness? Haven't I learned again today, for the hundredth time, just how much I'm worth? Won't I torment her to death!"

I stood in the snow, peering into the dull darkness, and thought about that.

"And won't it be better, yes, better," I fancied later, back at home, stifling the living pain in my heart with fantasies, "won't it be better if she now carries an insult away with her forever? An insult—but this is purification; it's the most stinging and painful consciousness! By tomorrow I'd have already dirtied her soul with myself and worn out her heart. But now the insult will never die in her, and however vile the dirt that awaits her—the insult will elevate and purify her . . . through hatred . . . hm . . . maybe also forgiveness . . . Though, by the way, will all that make it any easier for her?"

And in fact I'm now asking an idle question of my own: which is better—cheap happiness, or lofty suffering? Well, which is better?

Such were my reveries as I sat at home that evening, barely alive from the pain in my soul. Never before had I endured so much suffering and repentance; but could there have been even the slightest doubt, as I went running out of the apartment, that I would turn back halfway? Never have I met Liza again, or heard anything about her. I will also add that for a long time I remained pleased with the *phrase* about the usefulness of insult and hatred, even though I myself almost became sick then from anguish.

Even now, after so many years, all this comes out somehow *none too well* in my recollection. Many things come out none too well now in my recollections, but . . . shouldn't I just end my *Notes* here? I think it was a mistake to begin writing them. At least I've felt ashamed all the while I've been writing this *story*: so it's no longer literature, but corrective punishment. Because, for example, to tell long stories of how I defaulted on my life through moral corruption in a corner, through an insufficiency of milieu, through unaccustom to what is alive, and through vainglorious spite in the underground—is not interesting, by God; a novel needs a hero, and here there are *purposely* collected all the features for an antihero, and, in the first place, all this will produce a most unpleasant impression, because we've all grown unaccustomed to life, we're all lame, each of us more or less. We've even grown so unaccustomed that at times we feel a sort of loathing for real "living life," and therefore cannot bear to be reminded of it. For we've reached a point where we regard real "living life" almost as labor, almost as service, and we all agree in ourselves that it's better from a book. And why do we sometimes fuss about, why these caprices, these demands of ours? We ourselves don't know why. It would be the worse for us if our capricious demands were fulfilled. Go on, try giving us more independence, for example, unbind the hands of any one of us, broaden our range of activity, relax the tutelage, and we . . . but I assure you: we will immediately beg to be taken back under tutelage. I know you'll probably get angry with me for that, shout, stamp your feet: "Speak just for yourself and your miseries in the underground, and don't go saying '*we all*.' " Excuse me, gentlemen, but I am not justifying myself with this *allishness*. As far as I myself am concerned, I have merely carried to an extreme in my life what you have not dared to carry even halfway, and, what's more, you've taken your cowardice for good sense, and found comfort in thus deceiving yourselves. So that I, perhaps, come out even more "living" than you. Take a closer look! We don't even know where the living lives now, or what it is, or what it's called! Leave us to ourselves, without a book, and we'll immediately get confused, lost—we won't know what to join, what to hold to, what to love and what to hate, what to respect and what to despise. It's a burden for us even to be men—men with real, *our own* bodies and blood; we're ashamed of it, we consider it a disgrace, and keep trying to be some unprecedented omni-men. We're stillborn, and have long ceased to be born of living fathers, and we like this more and more. We're acquiring a taste for it. Soon we'll contrive to be born somehow from an idea. But enough; I don't want to write any more "from Underground" . . .

HOWEVER, the "notes" of this paradoxalist do not end here. He could not help himself and went on. But it also seems to us that this may be a good place to stop.

Notes

PART I: *Underground*

1. Collegiate assessor was the eighth of the fourteen ranks in the Imperial Russian civil service, equivalent to the military rank of major. The narrator had attained this rank by the time he quit the service, a year before writing his "notes" (1864), not at the time of the episodes he describes in Part II (1848–50).

2. The language here is biblical, reminiscent of many passages in the Psalms, the Book of Job, and the Gospels in which the righteous man is confronted by skeptical critics. Isaiah 19:11 refers specifically to the "wise counsellors" of Pharaoh; "waggers of heads" are mentioned in Matthew 27:39 and Mark 15:29.

3. This combination of terms goes back to such eighteenth-century treatises as *A Philosophical Enquiry into the Origin of Our Ideas of the Sublime and Beautiful* (1757), by the Anglo-Irish writer and statesman Edmund Burke (1729–97), and *Observations on the Feeling of the Beautiful and the Sublime* (1764), by the German philosopher Immanuel Kant (1724–1804). The Russian phrase, replacing "sublime" with the less rhetorical "lofty," became a critical commonplace in the 1840s, but acquired an ironic tone in the utilitarian and anti-aesthetic 1860s.

4. "The man of nature and truth" (French), Dostoevsky's mocking distortion of a sentence from the prefatory note of *Confessions* by the French philosopher and novelist Jean-Jacques Rousseau (1712–78): "Here is the only portrait of a man, painted exactly from nature and in all its truth, that exists and probably ever will exist."

5. Glancing references are made here to "Darwinism" and to the theory of "enlightened self-interest" put forward by the English utilitarians in the 1830s and -40s. Darwin avoided the question of human

evolution from other animals in his *Origin of Species* (1859); not so
T. H. Huxley (1825–95), whose book *Man's Place in Nature* (1863)
openly stated the case. A Russian translation of this book was published early in 1864, just as Dostoevsky was writing *Notes from
Underground*.

6. According to the *General Address Book* of Petersburg, there
were eight dentists named Wagenheim practicing in the city at the
time.

7. In fact, the phrase was characteristic of articles published in *Time*
and *Epoch*, magazines edited by Dostoevsky and his brother Mikhail
in 1861–65.

8. A "no-account" or "rascal" (French), from the German *Schnapp-
hahn*, a pilferer.

9. The Russian genre painter N. N. Ge (1831–94) exhibited a painting entitled *The Last Supper* at the Academy of Art in 1863. Dostoevsky detested the painting, and here takes advantage of the fact that the
artist's name (pronounced almost like the English word "gay") sounds
the same as the first letter—often used as a genteel euphemism—of the
Russian word *govno*, "shit." Hence the odd structure of the sentence.

10. Dostoevsky's ideological opponent M. E. Saltykov-Shchedrin
(1826–89) published an article with this title in the liberal monthly
The Contemporary (1863, no. 7). Dostoevsky pokes fun at him by
taking the title literally. Saltykov-Shchedrin had written an article
praising Ge's *Last Supper* for the same journal (1863, no. 11).

11. The English historian Henry Thomas Buckle (1821–62), in his
History of Civilization in England (1857–61), formulated the idea that
the development of civilization leads to the cessation of war between
nations.

12. The wars of the "great" Napoleon (1769–1821) are well known.
His nephew Napoleon III (1808–73; emperor 1852–70) started the
Crimean War against Russia (1854–56), took Cochin China for France
(1859–62), intervened in Mexico on the losing side of the emperor
Maximilian, and finally declared war on Prussia (1870), which led to
his capitulation and removal from power. At the time that Dostoevsky
was writing *Notes from Underground*, the North American union
was enduring the test of the Civil War, and Prussia was at war with
Denmark over possession of the province of Schleswig-Holstein,
which had been under Danish hegemony since 1773.

13. Attila (406?–53), "the Scourge of God," king of the Huns, led
devastating military campaigns against the Eastern Roman Empire,

Persia, and Gaul, before he was defeated near Chalons in 451 and driven back across the Danube. Stepan Timofeevich ("Stenka") Razin (?–1671), a Don Cossack, led a peasant uprising in Russia (1667–71), which made him a popular hero.

14. The metaphor of the piano key may go back to the French materialist philosopher and writer Denis Diderot (1713–84), who wrote in his *Conversation Between D'Alembert and Diderot* (1769): "We are instruments endowed with sense and memory. Our senses are piano keys upon which surrounding nature plays, and which often play upon themselves."

15. The "crystal palace" is an allusion to "The Fourth Dream of Vera Pavlovna" from the novel *What Is to Be Done?* (1863), by N. G. Chernyshevsky (1828–89), one of Dostoevsky's main ideological enemies and the target of much of the satire in *Notes from Underground*. Chernyshevsky's thought combined the humanitarian socialism of the 1840s with the utilitarianism of the 1860s. This chapter of *Notes* attacks the theory of "rational egoism" set forth in Chernyshevsky's *The Anthropological Principle in Philosophy* (1860); the episodes of the "bumped officer" and the "rescued prostitute" in Part II of *Notes* are to some extent reversed parodies of episodes from *What Is to Be Done?* Chernyshevsky's "crystal palace," a vision of the ideal living space for the future utopian communist society, based on the "phalanstery" defined by the French utopian socialist Charles Fourier (1772–1837), drew its physical details from the cast-iron and glass pavilion designed by Sir Joseph Paxton for the London Exposition of 1851.

16. Dostoevsky first heard of the bird Kagan, a folkloric bringer of happiness, during his imprisonment in Omsk (1849–53).

17. The Colossus of Rhodes, a 100-foot-high statue of Helios, the sun god, made in 280 B.C., stood in the harbor of the Greek island of Rhodes; it was one of the seven wonders of the ancient world. A. E. Anaevsky (1788–1866), a hack writer, was the object of much mockery in the press of the 1840s–60s.

18. "To domestic animals" (French).

19. The "fig" (referred to in chapter VIII by the narrator's supposed listeners) is a rude gesture made by inserting the thumb between the closed fingers of the fist. The "fig in the pocket" is a covert form of the same gesture, widely used in Russia, especially by intellectuals during the Soviet period, as an expression of dissent.

20. See Psalm 137:5: "If I forget you, O Jerusalem, let my right hand wither!" (Revised Standard Version).

21. In his book *On Germany*, the German poet Heinrich Heine (1797–1856) wrote: "The composition of one's own character description would be not only an awkward task but quite simply impossible ... However strong his wish to be sincere, no man is capable of telling the truth about himself." In the same book, Heine insists that Rousseau, in his *Confessions*, "makes false avowals, in order to hide his real doings behind them."

22. In his *Dostoevsky: The Stir of Liberation, 1860–1865*, Joseph Frank, drawing attention to an 1849 article in which the Russian critic P. V. Annenkov points to "wet snow" as a common meteorological condition in descriptions of Petersburg by writers of the natural school, suggests that Dostoevsky uses the same "wet snow" here to evoke both the atmosphere of the period he is going to write about (the late 1840s) and the naive assumptions of its literature, which he himself had shared.

PART II: *Apropos of the Wet Snow*

1. Dostoevsky's relations with N. A. Nekrasov (1821–78), poet, liberal social critic, and editor of *The Contemporary*, were respectful but often strained. The poem quoted here, written in 1845, tells the story of a rescued prostitute.

2. Kostanzhoglo, an exemplary manager and landowner, appears in the unfinished second part of *Dead Souls* by Nikolai Gogol (1809–52). Pyotr Ivanovich Aduyev, from the novel *An Ordinary Story* (1847) by Ivan Goncharov (1812–91), is distinguished by his common sense and practicality.

3. Weimar, in the German province of Thuringia, became an important intellectual center in the late eighteenth and early nineteenth centuries owing to the influence of its most famous citizen, the poet Johann Wolfgang von Goethe (1749–1832). The Schwarzwald, or Black Forest, in southwestern Germany, is a "romantic" region of hills and woodlands separated from France by the Rhine valley.

4. Poprishchin, hero of Gogol's *Diary of a Madman* (1835), is a petty clerk who finally goes mad and imagines he is the king of Spain.

5. Lieutenant Pirogov, one of the heroes of Gogol's *Nevsky Prospect* (1835), after being whipped by an irate German husband, wants to complain against him to the authorities.

6. The exposé (Dostoevsky ironically distorts the spelling here)

became a common journalistic phenomenon only in the 1860s; thus the narrator was somewhat precocious in his wish to "expose" his officer. *Fatherland Notes*, a liberal monthly founded in Petersburg in 1818, published during the sixty-six years of its existence some of the most important writers of the age, including Lermontov, Nekrasov, Ostrovsky, and Dostoevsky himself.

7. The French *superflu*, meaning "in excess," "unnecessary," or "useless," is here taken to mean "ultra-refined." Nozdryov in Gogol's *Dead Souls* uses the word in the same sense.

8. A covered shopping area in the center of Petersburg, still in existence and still so called.

9. That is, suggestive of the gloomy, proud, world-weary hero of the verse drama *Manfred* (1817) by George Gordon, Lord Byron (1788–1824).

10. In 1805, Napoleon defeated a joint Austrian-Russian army at Austerlitz in Moravia. However, in *Voyage to Icaria* (1840), a utopian communist novel by the French publicist Etienne Cabet (1788–1856), a philanthropic reformer also defeats a coalition of retrograde kings at Austerlitz.

11. The narrator's further imaginings also have Napoleonic touches: Pope Pius VII excommunicated Napoleon in 1809, after which the emperor held him virtually captive until 1814; the Villa Borghese, built by Scipione Borghese in 1615 as a summer house on the outskirts of Rome, belonged in 1806 to Camillo Borghese, who married Napoleon's sister Paulina. Lake Como is normally situated in the Italian Alps, near the Swiss border.

12. An intersection in Petersburg, still so called, where four streets come together to form five corners.

13. Before the emancipation of the serfs in 1861, Russian estates were valuated in terms of the number of "souls" (adult male serfs) living on them.

14. "Right as a lord" (French), referring to the right of the feudal lord, when one of his serfs married, to spend the first night with the bride.

15. Silvio, hero of "The Shot" (1830), a short story by the poet Alexander Pushkin (1799–1837), devotes his life to the idea of revenge and finally triumphs over his adversary. A similar role is played by the character Incognito in *Masquerade*, a drama by Mikhail Lermontov (1814–41).

16. In his enthusiasm, the narrator begins to speak in the words of

the biblical Creator: "Then God said, 'Let us make man in our image, after our likeness' " (Genesis 1:26).

17. In the 1840s, the French novelist George Sand (1804–76) was particularly admired in Russia for her social and humanitarian concerns.

18. The last lines of the Nekrasov poem quoted as epigraph to Part II.

19. "Furnished rooms" (French), which, while making a servant unnecessary, would expose the narrator to the presence of other lodgers.

VINTAGE CLASSICS

penguin.co.uk/vintage